The Empty House

FIONA KELLY

Special thanks to Allan Frewin Jones

CATNIP BOOKS
Published by Catnip Publishing Ltd.
14 Greville Street
London
EC1N 8SB

This edition published 2007
1 3 5 7 9 10 8 6 4 2

Text copyright © 1995 by Working Partners Ltd
Original series created by Ben M. Baglio

A CIP catalogue record for this book is available from the British Library

ISBN 978-1-84647-038-7

Printed in Poland

www.catnippublishing.co.uk

The Empty House

Contents

1

The new house

'Help!' Holly Adams yelled, as the heavy weight came thumping down on top of her. It knocked her off her feet and flattened her on the stairs. 'Help! I'm being *crushed*!'

She struggled under the suffocating weight, finally managing to drag herself up above the end of the mattress. Her long brown hair was over her face.

Lower down the stairs, her two friends were doubled up with laughter.

'I told you to watch where you were going,' said Josh Hamilton. Amy Hunt, her long blonde hair tied back with an elastic band, was leaning against the banister rail, helpless with laughter.

'Calm down, you three,' Mr Hamilton said from the hallway. 'We don't want any accidents.' He was carrying the television set.

'I think we've just had one,' said Josh. 'You OK, Holly?'

'Amy did that on purpose!' said Holly. 'I said *stop*!'

'Sorry,' said Amy, her round face split by a grin. 'I thought you said *shove*!'

'Just you be careful,' said Mr Hamilton. 'I'm beginning to wish I'd hired professional removal men, after all.' He carried the television set into the sitting-room.

The Hamiltons were moving house.

Holly, in her usual way of wanting to be in on everything, had volunteered herself and Amy to help with the move.

Holly and Amy were best friends. Both twelve years old, they had lived in the same part of North London all their lives. Josh, on the other hand, had only moved into the area a few months ago. He and his father had been renting a small flat. Now they were finally moving into a house of their own.

Or they *would be*, if the three friends could

manage to get Josh's mattress up the stairs to his bedroom.

'OK,' said Josh, hoping that just this once the two girls might follow his instructions. 'Let's try this again, shall we?'

Holly grabbed the top of the mattress.

'Right,' she puffed. 'When I say shove – *shove!*'

'Got you,' said Amy, squeezing in next to Josh as they both lifted the foot of the mattress in their arms.

'Shove!' said Holly.

They shoved. The mattress twisted and bounced as if it had a life of its own.

'Ow!' wailed Holly, as her heel caught on the stairs and she vanished under the mattress for a second time.

Amy's piercing laugh rang through the empty house.

Holly struggled to get free again. *There are times*, she thought, *when I wish I wasn't so quick to be helpful*!

Josh's bedroom looked like a left-luggage office

after a hurricane has struck. There were boxes and bags and suitcases piled all over the floor, and the furniture was all at strange angles and in odd places. But at least everything was finally in there!

As the three friends sat on the floor, eating fish and chips out of newspaper, they could hear bangs and thuds from downstairs. A couple of Mr Hamilton's friends were helping to move the really heavy furniture.

Holly and her two friends were taking a well-deserved break. They had been toiling away all morning and they were tired and dusty and red-faced from their exertions.

'Phew! I needed that!' said Holly, swigging from a Coke can.

'I need a shower,' said Amy. 'I'm all sticky and horrible.' She plucked at her T-shirt. 'I haven't worked this hard since ...' She paused, thinking. 'I haven't worked this hard *ever*!' she said. She looked at Josh. 'Next time you move, remind me to be somewhere else.'

'Next time?' said Josh. 'Are you kidding? We're not moving again, ever!' He looked unhappily round at his jumbled possessions. 'It's going to take me weeks to get all this lot back in order.'

'We'll help you,' said Amy. She pulled a big sheaf of papers out of a box. 'Where does this go?'

'Leave it!' yelled Josh. 'I'll do it. You'll mess up my system.' Josh had three or four big boxes heaped with notebooks and sheaves of closely written paper. He collected car number plates. He also collected coach and bus numbers. He had a whole stack of reference books. The two girls thought he was mad.

Not that Josh had had much time to pursue his hobby since he had encountered the two girls. Not since the three of them had set up the K.I.D.Z.

Holly and Amy had started the club, inspired by a book they had both read called *Harriet the Spy*. Harriet, who lives in New York, spends her time collecting information about the comings and goings of her friends and neighbours. Holly wanted to do something similar. She had an unquenchable thirst for mysteries – but until she, Amy and Josh had got together, all Holly's mysteries had been in books. These days, real-life mysteries seemed to erupt all around them.

The name had come from a newspaper

headline, *K.I.D.Z. Foil Bank Robbery*. That had been their first adventure.

Holly screwed up the empty fish-and-chip paper. She stood up, stretching her aching limbs.

'The garden won't need much doing to it,' she said, looking out of the window. Josh's room was on the first floor at the back of the house. The row of terraced houses was on the crest of a hill. The garden, a neat lawn bordered by flower-beds, sloped down to a rickety-looking wooden fence.

Josh looked over her shoulder. 'That's more than you can say about *that* one,' he said. Beyond the fence, the garden of the house directly behind was like a small jungle. The lawn was a mass of overgrown weeds and spiky grass-heads. Rose bushes and masses of rhododendron spread out of control amongst rubbish and debris. The house itself was obviously empty. It looked almost derelict. From her vantage point, Holly could see bare floorboards in the ground floor rooms.

'Who on earth lives there?' said Amy, coming up behind them. 'There's no furniture or anything. They must eat off the floor.'

'No one lives there,' said Josh.

'I can see that,' said Amy. 'I was *joking*.'

'It's number fourteen Roseway Road,' said Josh. 'I saw something about it in the estate agent's window when I was in there with my dad. It's up for auction in a few weeks.'

'Auction?' said Holly. 'What does that mean?'

'It means it's a dump,' said Josh. 'It means no building society or bank is prepared to lend anyone the money for a mortgage. Whoever buys it will have to pay cash, see?'

'Who'd pay cash for a tip like that?' said Amy.

Josh shrugged. 'Someone who's prepared to spend a lot of money on it and then sell it off, I suppose,' he said.

'And someone who's prepared to do a lot of work on the garden, too,' said Holly. 'Crumbs! You'd need a flame-thrower to get through that lot!' She stared across at the dusty, uncurtained windows. 'They'd need to clear out all those boxes as well.'

'What boxes?' said Josh.

'Those boxes,' said Holly, pointing towards a pair of glass-panelled doors at the back of the house. Planks and hunks of hardboard were piled against the outside of the doors, but through the glass a group of medium-sized boxes could be seen, stacked together on the floorboards.

'That's funny,' said Josh. 'They weren't there yesterday.'

'Maybe someone's moving in,' said Amy.

'They can't be,' said Josh. 'I told you, the auction's not for two weeks.'

'Whoever moved out last must have left them, then,' said Holly. 'I expect they're empty.'

Josh gave them a puzzled look. 'Dad and I were over here measuring up yesterday evening,' he said. 'I was in here working out where everything would go. I distinctly remember looking over there and thinking I was glad our house wasn't in such a bad state. And there were no boxes there then, I can tell you that.'

'You just didn't see them,' said Amy.

'I'd have seen them,' Josh said determinedly. 'If I can see them *now*, I'd have seen them yesterday evening.'

'So what?' said Amy. 'Who cares about a load of old boxes? Someone's just dumped them there.'

'Yes, but who?' said Holly.

'The man in the moon, for all I care,' said Amy. 'Josh? Have you finished with us for the day? Is there any chance of me going home and having a shower now?'

'Aren't you even a little bit intrigued?' Holly asked her.

'Intrigued?' said Amy. 'About empty boxes in an empty house? No, I'm not. I'm tired and dirty and I want to go home and have a good wash and change out of these sticky clothes.'

'You're sure we can't help you unpack?' Holly asked Josh.

'I'm certain,' said Josh. 'I spent two days packing everything in the right order. If I let you two loose on it, it'll be six months before I get my system sorted out again.'

Amy rolled her eyes. 'You and your weird hobbies,' she said.

'It's not *weird*,' Josh said, probably for the hundredth time. 'It's interesting.'

'If you say so,' said Amy, rubbing her nose. The disturbed dust of the move had been making her sneeze all morning. 'But right now, all I'm interested in is getting under a shower. Are you coming, Holly? Or are the pair of you going to spend the rest of the afternoon staring at those boxes over there?'

'I'm coming,' said Holly.

They picked their way through Josh's belongings and headed downstairs.

Through the open sitting-room door they saw Mr Hamilton and the two men who had been helping them move sitting on the couch, taking a break.

'We're off now,' Holly said.

'Thanks for all your help,' said Mr Hamilton.

'That's OK,' said Holly. 'Any time!'

'Holly!' said Amy. 'Don't say things like that!'

Mr Hamilton laughed. 'Don't worry,' he said. 'We'll be staying put for a while.'

'I'm glad to hear it,' said Amy.

The front door was wedged open and the large van in which they had moved all the Hamiltons' possessions was standing at the kerb.

'It's going to be great,' said Josh, as he walked with them to the end of the path. 'Plenty of room, at last! We've even set aside a small room just for my files and stuff. We're going to put up shelves and everything. I'm going to have my desk in there. I might even get a filing cabinet.'

'I'm sure you'll be very happy together,' said Amy. 'You and all your files.'

Holly looked at Josh with suddenly glowing eyes. 'You mean an extra room all to yourself?' she said. 'Hey, we could use it for our meetings. It could be like our own office! The K.I.D.Z. office!'

'I don't see why not,' said Josh, turning to go back inside.

This was something Holly had always longed for. A special room where they could meet. Not just a bedroom, but a private room where they could hold meetings and discuss things without interruption.

Josh's old bedroom had been too cramped for meeting up on a regular basis. When they met at Holly's house there was always the problem of Jamie, her pest of a younger brother, sticking his nose in. And at Amy's house there were her irritating older twin sisters to cope with.

Holly and Amy lived only a few streets away from each other, and as they walked along, Holly was already full of ideas for their new office.

'I tell you what would be really good,' she said. 'A great big map of London. We could have it up on the wall. And whenever anything happened, we could stick coloured marker pins in it.'

'And we could have one of those charts, like my mum's got in her office,' said Amy. 'Showing who's supposed to be doing what, and when. And I know where we can get one, too. There's a shop that sells stuff like that in Croftleigh Road. You know, where the market is.'

'Yes, I know it,' said Holly. 'Let's go there right now.'

'Wait a minute,' Amy said. 'Not *now*, Holly! I'm filthy. Look at me!'

Once Holly's enthusiasm was fired up, it was difficult to stop her. 'But, Amy—'

'Tomorrow!' interrupted Amy. 'We can go over there tomorrow. All the shops over there are open on a Sunday. We'll go over there with Josh in the morning, OK?'

Holly frowned. Tomorrow! She didn't want to have to wait until tomorrow. But then she thought how grubby she was herself after a morning of heavy removal work.

'OK,' she said with a smile. 'Tomorrow. And then we can start setting up the office! Brilliant! It'll be absolutely brilliant!'

2

Midnight torchlight

It was Sunday morning at Holly's house, and Holly was cooking scrambled eggs for the family. She'd found the recipe in a magazine. Eggs, milk, cheese, salt, pepper and chives. Cook until firm and serve on buttered toast.

'It's ready!' cried Holly. Mr and Mrs Adams were at either end of the table, the Sunday papers spread out in front of them. Jamie was busy with a pocket game machine that sent out a constant barrage of high-pitched beeps.

The newspapers were cleared away.

'This looks good,' said Mr Adams with a smile. 'Jamie! Come on, don't let it get cold.'

'What're these bits?' said Jamie, jabbing his

finger at the scrambled egg.

'Chives,' said Holly. 'They're nice.'

'They're not,' said Jamie. 'They're horrible. It looks like grass.'

'Eat!' said Mrs Adams sternly. 'If Holly's gone to the trouble of making it for us, you can at least give it a try.'

Jamie mumbled something about sheep food.

'Very nice,' said Mrs Adams. She looked at Holly. 'Are you going over to Josh's house today?'

'Later,' said Holly. 'First of all we're going to Croftleigh Road to pick up some stuff for our office.'

Mr Adams gave her a quizzical look. Holly explained about the spare room in Josh's new house.

'It's amazing,' Mr Adams said with a laugh. 'I spend all my life wishing I *wasn't* in an office, and Holly, here, can't wait to get into one.' Holly's father was a successful solicitor, but his real love was carpentry. He spent most of his free time in his workshop in the cellar.

'Are you sure Josh's father won't mind you invading his house like that?' said Mrs Adams.

Holly shook her head. 'There's plenty of room

there,' she said. 'We won't be in the way at all.'

Holly met up with Amy an hour or so later, and the two of them set off to pick up Josh. The house was still full of unopened boxes, and the buzz of an electric drill sounded from where Josh's father was already busy putting up some shelves.

'Got all your files sorted?' Amy asked.

'Not yet,' said Josh, as he closed the front door behind them. 'While we're out, Dad wants me to have a look for a second-hand DVD player.' He smiled. 'I've been on at him for ages to get one. There's a shop that sells second-hand stuff like that in Croftleigh Road. We can have a look in there.'

The three of them set off for Croftleigh Road. They came out of an alley between two shops and found the small street market right in front of them.

The electrical shop was called Square Deal. The three friends went inside to have a look round. There certainly was a lot of stuff in there:

televisions, DVD players, electric typewriters, word processors and mobile phones filled the racks.

A man stood behind a counter at the back of the shop, doing something to a small portable television set with a tiny screwdriver.

While Josh asked the man about a DVD, Holly and Amy browsed among the shelves.

The man showed Josh a few DVD players while Josh wrote down the details and prices.

'Well?' asked Amy as they left the shop. 'Did you see anything?'

'I think so,' said Josh. 'I'll have to report back to Dad, to see how much he wants to spend.'

Their next stop was at the office and stationery suppliers, a little way along the road.

Inside, they found exactly what they wanted: a huge wall map of the whole of London. The major streets were picked out in yellow, parks and open spaces in green. It was over a metre wide and about a metre high. *Exactly* what they wanted.

They pooled their money and bought it, using the little money they had left over for a small box of coloured pins.

'Now we're really in business,' said Holly as she

walked along with the map rolled under her arm. 'Let's get back and put it up.'

Holly didn't say so, but she was a little bit disappointed when she saw the size of their new room. It was a tiny boxroom right at the top of the house. Already, Josh's cartons almost filled it.

But at least it was their own room. A place where they could be sure of not being disturbed by her pesky brother and Amy's sarcastic sisters.

They spent most of the day sorting the room out. At least, Josh did. He wouldn't let the two girls touch his precious files, so they sat round happily chatting about all the things they could get up to in there, while he toiled away.

The map looked very professional up on the wall. Holly put three blue pins in it, marking out the streets where they lived.

'It's a pity we don't have any mysteries to solve right now,' said Amy, grinning as she watched the way Josh meticulously sorted his files into neat piles on the floor.

'There's always the mystery of why Josh keeps stacks and stacks of number plates,' said Holly.

'Ha, ha,' said Josh. He was used to being laughed at by the two girls, and he didn't really mind.

They arranged to hold their first meeting after school on Monday.

'Maybe by then,' Amy said to Josh as she and Holly left, 'you'll have got all your stuff out of the way and we'll actually have some room in there.'

Holly and Amy went to the Thomas Petheridge Comprehensive. Josh had been living in Highgate for only a few months and had been attending a school a long train journey away. But that was going to change very soon. Josh was transferring to Holly and Amy's school in a couple of weeks' time.

The girls were looking forward to that. Josh had always insisted that the girls shouldn't discuss K.I.D.Z. work when he wasn't with them. But soon, with Josh at the same school, they would be able to talk about their adventures all the time.

Not that the two girls had any shortage of other things to talk about at school. Especially as they co-edited the lower-school magazine, *The Tom-*

tom. It was only a few photocopied sheets which came out monthly, but Holly and Amy spent an enormous amount of their free time at school vetting articles and coming up with new ideas to make the magazine as interesting as possible.

Josh had his camera in his hand when they arrived at his house on Monday afternoon.

'I've been taking a whole lot of shots of the house,' he told them. 'I'm going to make a before-and-after portfolio, so that we'll be able to see how different the place looks once we've got it all sorted out and decorated.'

They went upstairs, stopping off at his bedroom so he could take a few snaps of the garden out of the window.

'Hey,' said Holly, looking out of the window. 'Those boxes have gone!'

Josh grinned. 'I was wondering if you'd spot that,' he said. 'Come on up to our office. I've got something even more interesting to tell you.'

Josh had pinned a notice on the door of their office:

PRIVATE
STRICTLY OUT OF BOUNDS
NO ENTRY

'Very impressive,' said Amy. 'I suppose *we're* allowed in, are we?'

'Only if you give the special knock,' said Josh. He rapped his knuckles on the door. *Tap ti-ti tap tap ... Tap tap!*

Amy giggled. She often found Josh and Holly's secret agent tactics comical.

Ignoring her, Josh opened the door and they went inside.

Their room was looking a lot tidier. Josh's desk was in there now and his files were all stacked out of the way against the wall.

'There's only one chair,' Amy pointed out. 'Where are we supposed to sit?'

'You could try the floor,' suggested Josh. 'I'll get some cushions up here later.'

The three of them sat on the floor.

'Well?' said Holly. 'What's the big news?'

'I was lying in bed last night,' Josh said with slow relish. 'I couldn't get off to sleep. I was thinking about how I am going to arrange my files once Dad's put the shelves up in here.'

'That'd put me to sleep in ten seconds flat,' said Amy.

'*Five* seconds,' added Holly.

'Do you want to hear about this or not?' asked Josh.

'Go on, then,' said Holly. 'You were lying awake last night. Then what?'

'I thought I heard a noise out the back,' said Josh. 'It's really quiet here at night. So I had a look out of my window. And guess what I saw?'

'I know,' said Amy. 'There was a whole gang of fairies having a barbecue at the bottom of your garden.'

'I saw *lights* in that empty house,' Josh said, ignoring Amy. 'I don't mean electric lights. Not normal house lights. It looked like torchlight. It sort of came and went, as if someone was creeping about in there.'

'Did you see anyone?' asked Holly.

'Well, yes − sort of,' said Josh. 'That was the really strange bit. It was upstairs. The torchlight was moving round up there, and then there was this sudden flash.' Josh made an explosive gesture with both hands. 'It was only for a split second. A really bright light. And I saw two silhouettes − just for an instant.' He looked at the two girls.

'Wow,' breathed Amy. 'Did you see anything else?'

'No,' said Josh. 'After the flash of light, the torchlight carried on moving round upstairs for about ten minutes and then it went out. I kept watch for a while longer, but nothing else happened. Except that when I looked out this morning all those boxes were gone.' He looked at the two girls. 'Is that strange, or what?'

'Maybe it's squatters,' said Holly. 'You know, people who saw the house was empty and just moved in illegally.'

'Why would squatters creep about at midnight moving boxes?' said Josh.

'I know,' said Amy. 'It was a *murder*. Someone lured a victim there. Then he stole all their money, chopped them into little bits and hid them in the boxes.'

'You are the most gruesome person in the *world*!' said Holly. 'You've got a seriously warped mind, Amy, do you know that?'

Amy grinned. 'It was just a theory,' she said.

'I don't think it was anything like that,' said Josh. 'But I think I know what the bright light was. It was a flash-bulb from a camera. I'm sure there's something strange going on over there. And it's got something to do with those boxes.'

'You mean something criminal?' asked Holly.

'Hey, maybe it's a spy ring?' her eyes shone as her imagination started to work. 'I've got it! Some foreign power has sent its top spies over here to gather information. Those boxes are probably full of radio transmitters and bugging devices. And cameras with enormous zoom lenses.'

'Just like in *Spyglass*,' said Amy. *Spyglass* was their favourite television programme. Every week the K.I.D.Z. were glued to the screen, breathlessly following the adventures of Secret Agent John Raven. 'They might have long-distance listening devices, too.' She glanced towards the window. 'We'd better keep our voices down. They could be listening to us *right now!*'

'I wouldn't have thought so,' said Josh. 'I can't really see a foreign power sending people all the way over here to listen to *you*.'

'But you agree it *might* be spies?' said Holly.

'Not really,' said Josh. 'But I think we could do some investigating.' He grinned. 'After all, that's what we set up the K.I.D.Z. for, wasn't it? To investigate strange things like this.'

'What sort of investigating could we do?' asked Amy. 'If all this goes on at night, I don't see what we can do about it.'

'I'm going to keep watch,' Josh said firmly. 'All night, if I have to.'

'Rather you than me,' said Amy. 'I bet you fall asleep.'

'I won't!' Josh protested.

'OK,' said Holly. 'You keep watch on the place tonight, Josh. We'll come over here after school tomorrow, and you can fill us in on anything you see.'

'Will do,' said Josh.

'*If* you keep awake,' said Amy.

'I'll keep awake, all right,' said Josh. 'Don't worry about that! I shan't close my eyes for a *second*!'

3

Footprints in the dust

It was the week in which *The Tom-tom* came out, and, as usual, all Holly and Amy's spare time at school was being taken up in last-minute preparations for the magazine.

The two girls were in the resource room. Holly was sitting at the word processor while Amy watched over her shoulder.

'Wouldn't it be quicker if you used more than two fingers?' Amy asked as Holly tapped at the keyboard.

'It'd be quicker if you weren't breathing down my neck,' said Holly. 'Can't you find something useful to do? Think up a couple of jokes for the funny section.'

'We've got plenty,' said Amy. Amy was in charge of the joke page. She picked up a scrap of paper. 'What about this one? What goes black-white-black-white-black-white?'

'I don't know,' said Holly, trying to concentrate on her typing.

'A penguin rolling down a hill,' said Amy.

Holly groaned.

'Have you remembered that notice Mr Taylor gave us?' asked Amy. Mr Taylor was the head teacher. He frequently used *The Tom-tom* to get information round the school.

'Front page,' said Holly, scrolling the screen back to page one.

' "It's fund-raising time again!" ' Holly read.

' "Mr Taylor has asked us to remind you that the official fund-raising campaign starts this week. We are collecting money for some additional computer terminals for the school. Anyone with any brilliant ideas for ways of raising money should contact Miss Springfield in the secretary's office. Come on, you lot, think up some ideas! We need those terminals, and we need them *now!*" '

'That should do the trick,' said Amy. 'Have you come up with any ideas?'

'Not yet,' said Holly.

'We could kidnap Mrs Jarman and hold her to ransom,' suggested Amy. Mrs Jarman was a terrifying games teacher. She was known as Queen Kong.

'Who'd pay to get *her* back?' asked Holly. 'People would pay to get *rid* of her, maybe.'

Holly scrolled the screen back to where she had left off and began to type in the results of recent netball matches.

Amy took out her red pen and did a final edit of the jokes page. One thing *The Tom-tom* was never short of were terrible jokes handed in by the rest of the lower school.

'I wonder how Josh got on last night,' said Holly.

'He'll have fallen asleep,' said Amy. 'You can bet on it.'

'No he won't,' said Holly. 'Knowing Josh he'll have spent half the night staring out of that window. You know what he's like.'

'Is it a bet, then?' asked Amy. 'Fifty pence says he was fast asleep by ten o'clock.'

'You're on,' said Holly. 'That'll be the easiest fifty pence I ever make. It can go towards the computer.'

'Fifty pence!' said Amy with a grin. 'Hand it over, Holly.'

They were in their office in Josh's house that afternoon. The good news was that Josh had brought up some cushions for them to sit on. The bad news, especially for Holly, was that he had admitted falling asleep after about half an hour of watching.

'This moving house business is really exhausting,' Josh explained, his face red with shame. 'I couldn't keep my eyes open.'

'You should have propped them open with matchsticks,' Holly complained. 'That's the last time I trust you!'

'I woke up later,' said Josh. 'There were some cats having a yowling competition. They sound really weird, you know, in the middle of the night. I had a look out of the window.'

'Any lights in the house?' Holly asked hopefully.

'Nope,' said Josh. 'But I could *almost* swear I saw someone moving about in the garden over there.

It was dead dark, but I'm sure I saw something move.'

'Yes,' said Amy. 'Courting cats, I expect.'

'So now what do we do?' asked Holly, frowning at Josh. 'It doesn't look like we can trust you to keep watch.'

'Why don't we just go round there?' suggested Amy. 'You never know, we might spot something through the front windows. You know, traces of dried blood where the landlord chopped up—'

'Amy!' exclaimed Holly. 'Will you shut up about that! We're looking for spies, not maniacs with choppers. Murderers don't take photos, for heaven's sake! But you're right about one thing. We ought to go and have a look over there.'

They had put a red pin in the map to show where the empty house was. Red for mystery.

They headed down the street, turning left down the hill and then left again into Roseway Road. It was a street of two-storey houses, smaller and not as old as the house where Josh lived. Round bay windows looked out over narrow front gardens, although many of the gardens had been concreted over or only showed a few shrubs behind their low brick walls.

The empty house was easy to spot. Number fourteen. There was a large sign attached to the gate-post. It read *House for Auction* then the date of the auction and a telephone number for enquiries underneath. Not that it would have been difficult to spot the house, even without the sign. There was rubbish in the front area and the windows were bare of the net curtains which hung across the majority of the other houses' windows.

Someone with green fingers had obviously owned the house at some point, because there was a trellis to one side of the sunken front doorway, and an out-of-control climbing plant hung half-across the entrance, covered in tiny white flowers.

'That's a jasmine plant,' said Amy. 'It grows like crazy if you don't keep it under control.'

'Anyone got a pair of shears?' asked Josh, as he pushed the hanging tendrils aside and stepped up into the shadowy doorway.

Holly picked her way through the rubbish and peered through the gaping bay window.

'Nothing here,' she said. The room beyond was bare. Holly thought it looked terribly sad. There were dusty floorboards, and cobwebs over the ceiling. Lighter patches showed on the wallpaper where pictures had once hung. A naked bulb hung from the ceiling rose.

'Poor house,' she said. 'It needs a family to bring it back to life.'

She went to join her two friends in the doorway. Josh was trying to see through the door's frosted-glass panels. Two further glass panels were set into the sides of the door frame.

Amy pushed the doorbell. There was no sound.

'It's probably linked up to the electrics,' said Josh. 'That would all have been cut off when the last people moved out.' He crouched down and pushed at the letterbox. It opened with a creak.

'Anything?' asked Holly.

'A few letters and stuff,' said Josh, angling himself to try and see into the hallway. 'It's probably just junk mail.'

The glass in the side panels was clearer than in the door itself. Holly pulled her sleeve down over her hand, to give the dusty glass a quick wipe in the hope of seeing more clearly.

'Oh, crumbs!' she gasped. As she had pressed the heel of her hand against the glass panel, it had shifted inwards from one side. Holly winced, expecting the whole panel to come crashing down into the hall. But it didn't. It was held by a strip of wood on one side.

'You vandal!' said Amy. 'I saw you do that!'

'It wasn't *me*,' said Holly. 'I hardly touched it. It was already loose. Someone's taken out the strips of wood that should be holding it in place.' She gave the glass panel a tentative push with her finger and it scraped a little further open, leaving a small gap.

'Anyone could get in,' said Josh. 'All you'd need to do is reach through and I bet you could open the door.'

The three of them looked at one another.

'Should we?' said Holly.

'We could,' said Josh.

'Why not?' said Amy.

'Isn't it a bit like breaking in?' said Holly. 'I mean, we'd be trespassing.'

'Only if we were caught,' said Amy. 'And even then, we'd probably only get a good telling-off by the police.'

'Thanks,' said Holly. 'That's a great comfort.'

'You know what they say,' said Josh. '*Who dares wins*.'

Holly gave him a dubious look. 'Who says that?'

'I don't remember,' said Josh. 'But I know *someone* says it. And we're never going to catch any spies if we don't take a few risks.'

Holly looked at him. 'You really think it might be spies?'

'Well, whoever they were, they had a camera,' said Josh. 'And there's only one way to find out what they were up to.'

'Come on,' urged Amy. 'Let's do it. We could be in and out before anyone saw us. And if there really is something screwy going on in there ...' Her voice trailed off. She didn't need to say any more. They were all thinking the same thing: strange night-time lights in an empty house was just too good a mystery for the K.I.D.Z. to ignore.

Amy didn't wait for any further discussion. She pushed her hand through the narrow gap and a second later the front door creaked open.

'OK,' said Josh. 'In and out as quick as we can, right?'

He pushed the door open and stepped into the dusty hallway. Bare stairs led up to the top floor. Two doors stood open from the hall.

Amy sneezed. Holly nearly jumped out of her skin.

'Sorry,' said Amy. 'I'm allergic to house dust.'

Josh closed the door behind them and pushed the glass panel back into place. 'Just in case,' he said.

'In case of what?' asked Holly.

Josh shrugged. 'In case someone comes by and sees that the door is open,' he said. 'Hey! Look!'

The two girls followed the line of his pointing finger. The floorboards were thick with dust beyond the scattering of unwanted envelopes and local free papers.

'Someone's been in here,' said Holly. They could all see the way the dust had been disturbed. There were no actual footprints, but there were clear scuffings and scrapings in the dust to show that the house had recently been entered.

The trail of disturbed grime led along the hall and out through the furthest open door.

They followed the marks.

'Someone's been upstairs as well,' said Holly.

Josh nodded. 'I told you I saw the lights upstairs, didn't I?' he said.

They followed the marks of passing feet into the back room.

'This is the room you can see from your house,' said Holly. It was an empty room with French windows overlooking the wilderness that had once been a garden.

'No more boxes,' said Amy, rubbing her nose as the dust of the abandoned house threatened another sneeze. In the filtering sunlight they could see tiny specks of dust hanging in the air.

'Who's for investigating upstairs?' asked Holly.

'We're here now,' said Josh. 'We might as well have a good look round.'

A sound from the hallway froze them where they stood.

In the emptiness of the house, the sound was horribly clear.

The chink and rattle of a key being put in the lock of the front door.

'Can we get out the back way?' whispered Holly.

They tiptoed towards the French windows. Holly had her fingers on the door handle when the tickling in Amy's nose became too much for her.

'*Atishoo!*' sneezed Amy. 'Oh, crumbs! Sorry! *Atishoo!*'

Holly and Josh stared at her in horror.

'Who's there?' shouted a voice from the hallway.

The three friends stared at one another.

They were well and truly caught!

4

Now you see it, now you don't

A smartly dressed young woman came storming into the back room of the old house. Her blonde hair was cut severely short and her piercing blue eyes stared at the three friends from behind red-framed spectacles. She was carrying a large bunch of keys in one hand and a briefcase in the other.

The clicking of her heels came to an ominous stop as she regarded Holly and her friends with knitted eyebrows.

'How did you get in here?' she demanded.

'Through the front door,' said Holly, her heart

sinking. She already had visions of being marched off to the police station. Her mother would have plenty to say about *that*, she was sure. 'We weren't doing any harm,' she added.

'How dare you break in here,' said the woman. 'This is private property.' Her icy stare was unnerving. 'Do you know what that means?'

'Of course we do,' Amy said fearlessly. 'We were only having a look round. And we didn't break anything to get in here, either.'

Good old Amy, thought Holly. *She's not scared of anything*. And what she said was true enough – they hadn't broken anything. The glass pane had already been loosened.

'Do you mean the front door wasn't locked?' asked the woman. 'Is that what you're telling me?'

'I just pushed the door,' said Josh. 'And it came open.' That was true. Josh had pushed the door open after Amy had unlocked it.

Holly was about to mention the loose panel when Josh continued. 'Whoever owns this place ought to be more careful about security,' he said. 'Anyone could have got in.'

'Is this your house?' asked Amy.

'No,' said the woman. 'I work for the estate agent.' The severity of her expression had softened a little. 'You had no business being in the doorway in the first place,' she said.

'Sorry,' said Holly. 'We saw the place was empty. We didn't think anyone would mind.' She nodded towards Josh. 'He saw this place mentioned in the estate agent's office. His father was looking for a house. We just thought we'd come and check this one out.'

'That's not the way to go about it,' said the woman. 'You should have made an appointment. I can't just have people wandering in and out of properties when they feel like it.'

'Sorry,' said Josh. 'We didn't realise.'

Whatever the woman had intended to say next was interrupted by a hammering on the front door.

'Hello? Hello in there!' A man's voice. Footsteps sounded down the hall and an elderly man appeared in the doorway.

'Are you from the estate agent's?' the man demanded. He gave the three friends a brief glance before focusing his eyes on the woman. 'I've been wanting to catch you for weeks. I demand to know how long it is going to take for this property to be sold. It's an eyesore. What are you doing about it, eh?'

'And you are?' asked the woman.

'Frazer. Sidney Frazer. I own the house next door,' said the man. 'Do you realise this property has been empty for over six months? That garden out there is completely out of control. It's a disgrace.' He glared at the three friends. 'And what are these children doing in here? Causing mischief, I expect.'

'No, we aren't,' said Amy.

'Children are always causing mischief,' said the old man. 'Or *worse*. There have been a lot of burglaries round here recently.' He stared meaningfully at the three. 'Mrs Milligan at number twenty-three was burgled only last week.'

'We're not burglars!' Amy snapped. 'What kind of an idiot burglar would come into an empty house? We were just having a look round.'

'Exactly!' said Mr Frazer. 'And that's what happens when houses are left empty. They attract undesirables!'

Amy glared at the unpleasant old man. 'Can we go now?' she said. 'I don't think this is the sort of street Josh and his father would want to live in anyway.'

'Yes,' said the woman. 'Go! And don't let me catch you anywhere near this place again, or you'll be in real trouble.' She looked at Josh. 'If your father wants to view this property, he will have to make an appointment.'

'I don't think he'll bother,' said Josh. 'He wants a place with friendly neighbours. Thanks all the same.'

Mr Frazer made a 'harrumph' noise as they walked past him.

Holly and her friends were surprised to see yet another man at the front door. A man in his twenties, wearing overalls. He was staring at the open door with a puzzled, uneasy look on his face.

'What are you lot doing in here?' said the man. Before they had time to answer, the estate agent came marching into the hall, her heels clicking.

'Can I help you?' she asked.

The man looked past the three friends. 'I'm from the electricity board,' he said. 'I've come to read the meter.'

'Don't be ridiculous,' said the woman. 'The

electricity was cut off in this property six months ago.'

Holly could tell from the way the man's eyes shifted that he was doing some speedy thinking.

'Is this fourteen Acacia Road?' he said.

'Fourteen *Roseway* Road,' said the woman.

'I've got the wrong place,' said the man.

'So it would seem,' said the woman. 'Acacia Road runs parallel to this one, further down the hill.'

'Thanks,' said the man. 'Sorry to bother you.' He made a hasty retreat, got into a car and drove away.

Holly led her friends out from under the dangling jasmine. As they came to the pavement, they heard Mr Frazer speaking.

'I want something done about the garden, and I want it done *now*.'

'What a lovely person to have as a next-door neighbour,' said Amy. 'I bet you're glad you're not moving in here, Josh.'

Holly waited until they were out of earshot of the house.

'He wasn't from the electricity board,' she said. 'They drive around in official vans. He was just in an ordinary car.'

'So who was he?' asked Josh.

'I think it's time we went back to our office and had a proper think about this,' said Holly. She thought she sounded very professional.

'We talked our way out of trouble pretty well back there,' Amy said as they walked along. 'Don't you think we should have told her about the loose panel, though?'

'I was going to when Josh interrupted me,' said Holly.

'Look,' said Josh. 'If we'd told her, she'd have got it fixed, wouldn't she?'

'I suppose she would,' said Holly.

'And then whoever's creeping about the house in the middle of the night wouldn't be able to get in, would they?' said Josh. 'Our mystery would be over almost before it began. You know what it's like once adults get involved. This is *our* mystery, and we're going to solve it.'

'Good thinking, Sherlock,' said Amy. 'Why give up a good mystery without a fight?'

Josh grinned. 'You mean you agree with me?' he said.

'Of course,' said Holly. 'Don't look so surprised.'

'But you two hardly ever agree with anything I say,' said Josh.

'We do when you're right,' said Amy. 'Can we help it if you're not right very often?'

They took a quick detour to the chemist's on their way back to Josh's house, so that he could pick up the photographs he had taken of his new home.

'OK,' said Holly, once they were safely behind the closed door of their office. 'Let's think this through. Boxes appear in an empty house, and then vanish in the middle of the night. That same night, Josh sees lights in the house. And the flash of a camera. A man turns up at the house, pretending to be from the electricity board, and does a disappearing act as soon as he sees there are people there.' She was writing in her notebook as she spoke. 'I'm going to call that fake meter reader Sparky,' she said. She wrote it down. *Code-name: Sparky*.

'I wish we knew what was in those boxes,' said Amy.

'There's definitely something peculiar going on in there,' said Holly. 'I'm more convinced than ever, now. It may not be a spy ring, but I'll bet it's something sneaky. Something that no one is supposed to know about.'

'It's a pity we got caught before we could have a proper look round,' said Amy. 'Josh, you said the lights were upstairs, didn't you? Ahem, Josh! Are you paying attention?'

Josh looked up from flipping through his photographs. 'Yes,' he said. 'I'm listening.'

'Well?' asked Amy.

'Well what?' asked Josh. 'Sorry, I was just – oh! That's odd. Take a look at this.'

He held out one of the photographs to the girls. It was a shot of the back garden, taken from his bedroom window. In the top half of the photograph, the overgrown garden beyond the back fence was visible, as well as a section of the empty house.

'Yes,' Holly said drily. 'Very nice.'

Josh grinned. 'You haven't spotted it, have you?' he said. 'Oh! Of course! You haven't looked out of my bedroom window recently.' He got up. 'Come with me,' he said. 'I want to show you something.'

They went to his room and stared out of the window.

'OK,' said Amy. 'What are we looking at?'

Holly looked from the photograph to the view out of the window. Josh had seen something. It was like one of those puzzles where you get two pictures side by side and have to discover ten differences between them.

'Got it!' shouted Holly. 'In the photo there's a lot of stuff piled up against the French windows, but the stuff isn't piled up there now.'

'Oh, yes,' said Amy. 'It's all on the grass. I see. So someone has used those French windows recently.'

'Didn't I tell you I thought I saw someone in the garden the other night?' said Josh. 'That proves it. And look, in the photo the door to that garden shed is open. But it's closed now. Someone has been in the shed.'

It was true. Over to one side of the garden stood a ramshackle old shed. In the photograph, the door was hanging wide open. But as they looked out of the window, they could see that the shed door was now tightly closed and held by an angled length of wood.

'Right,' said Holly, her eyes shining with excitement. 'That's our next job, then. To find out what's been going on in that garden!'

5

Breaking in

'We can't risk going back in that house,' said Josh.
'You heard what the woman said. We'd be in big
trouble if she caught us round there again.'

Amy nodded in agreement. 'She's not going
to believe we're just having a look round again,'
she said. Her face brightened. 'Unless we go over
there in disguise!'

'What sort of disguise?' said Josh. 'We're still
going to look like twelve-year-olds whatever we
do. Unless you fancy wobbling over there on stilts
and wearing a long coat. How do you think I'd
look in a false moustache?'

'Even dopier than you look right now,' said
Amy. 'And I don't suppose dark glasses and big

hats would fool anyone, either. You know, there are times when it's a real *pain* being young! If we were grown-up we could just put on wigs and funny voices and go round there pretending we wanted to buy the place.' She jumped up. 'Good afternoon,' she said in a deep voice. 'My name is Mrs Twitterington-Smythe.' She made a grand gesture towards Josh. 'And this is my butler, Perkins. I'd like to arrange to view number fourteen Roseway Road, my good woman. And hurry up about it, I'm having tea with the Lord Mayor this evening!'

Josh shook his head. 'You're batty,' he said.

'When you two have quite finished,' said Holly, 'I'd like to say something.'

Amy sat down. 'Mrs Twitterington-Smythe is all ears,' she gurgled.

'We don't have to go into the house again,' said Holly. 'All we need to do is hop over the back fence.'

'What?' said Josh. 'In broad daylight? With that estate-agent woman still lurking around? Not to mention the nosy neighbour from next door. They'd be all over us before we could move.'

'I wasn't thinking we should do it right now,'

said Holly. 'We could do it tomorrow afternoon.'

'But we'll be seen!' exclaimed Josh.

'Maybe,' Holly said coolly. 'Which is why we need to come up with a reasonable excuse.'

'I know,' said Amy. 'We could tell them we're practising for the inter-school hurdles championship. You know, leaping garden fences as part of our training routine.'

'Tennis,' said Holly. '*That's* our excuse. We can have a game of tennis in Josh's garden tomorrow afternoon. We could accidentally-on-purpose lob the ball over the back fence. No one could blame us for hopping over the fence to look for our ball, could they?' She looked at her two friends. 'Well?' she said. 'What do you say?'

'I can't play tennis,' said Josh.

'That's no problem,' said Holly. 'The ball's even more likely to get lost if you don't know what you're doing.'

'I haven't got a racket,' added Josh.

'I'll lend you one,' said Amy. 'And don't worry, with my brilliant power serve, that ball will be over the fence like a rocket!'

'Ow!' Josh yelled as the tennis ball bounced off the back of his head. 'I wasn't ready for it yet! I was doing up my shoelace!'

Amy gave a shriek of laughter. 'It wouldn't have made any difference if you *were* ready,' she yelled. 'You haven't hit one ball since we've been out here!'

It was the following afternoon. Holly and Amy had arrived at Josh's house with their rackets after school. The sun blazed down as the two girls ran rings round Josh. He had been right about one thing – he couldn't play tennis.

'Mr Hamilton to serve,' said Holly, who was temporary umpire. 'Miss Hunt leads two games to love in the first set. New balls, please.'

'We've only got one ball,' Amy reminded her.

'I know,' said Holly. 'But you're supposed to say "new balls, please" every now and then. It's how they do it on the telly. Josh, for heaven's sake, hold the racket properly. Anyone would think it was a *snake*, the way you're holding it!'

'Don't keep on at me,' complained Josh. 'I'm

doing my best. How do I serve again?'

'Chuck the ball in the air and wallop it,' said Amy. She bounced professionally from foot to foot in her white shorts and white T-shirt, her long hair flying.

Josh hurled the ball into the air and made a futile swipe at it. The two girls rocked with laughter as the ball fell unwalloped at his feet.

He threw his racket down.

'Misuse of racket,' yelled Holly. 'Game violation by Mr Hamilton. One point penalty. Love fifteen.'

'Oh, shut up,' said Josh. 'I'll be umpire. You two play. I thought the whole idea was to get that ball over the fence, not to make me look a complete idiot.'

'We can do both,' laughed Amy. 'No problem.' She moved down to the bottom of the garden and Holly prepared to serve.

The ball bounced and arched into the air.

Amy leaped into the air and returned the ball with a yell of triumph.

'You can't get past the mighty Hunt!' she said.

'You twit,' said Holly. 'That would have gone over the fence!'

'Oh! Sorry!' said Amy. 'I got carried away.'

'Just *leave* it next time,' said Holly. She served again, a much lower lob that bounced almost at Amy's feet. Amy ducked to avoid it, and the ball sailed over the fence.

'Oh dear,' said Amy. 'We seem to have lost our ball!'

'About time!' said Josh. 'Can we get on with it, now?'

They headed down to the bottom of the garden. Josh tested the strength of the fence. It wobbled alarmingly.

'It's going to collapse if we're not careful,' he said.

'Never!' said Holly. 'You're always looking for problems, Josh.' She bounced on her toes a couple of times, grabbed the top of the shoulder-high fence and hauled herself up on to it.

There was a creaking, cracking noise.

'Holly, careful!' wailed Amy.

But it was too late. With a loud crunching noise, an entire section of the fence broke away from its supporting posts and deposited Holly on her face in the adjoining garden.

'Brilliant!' said Josh. 'Absolutely brilliant, Holly!

Thanks a lot. My dad will be really pleased when he gets home and sees this.'

Holly picked herself up, brushing splinters of rotten wood off her clothes. 'It's OK, Josh,' she said. 'Don't worry. I haven't hurt myself. Thanks for asking.'

'I don't care about *you*,' said Josh. 'Look what you've done! I'll probably have to pay for this out of my allowance.'

Amy stepped on to the broken section of fence and over into the wild garden. The long, stringy grass reached up to her waist. 'At least we're in here now,' she said. She looked round at the houses on either side. 'And it doesn't look like anyone heard us, either.'

'We can prop the fence up when we come back out,' said Holly. 'No one will know the difference. I mean, come on, Josh, it would probably have fallen down all on its own, the state it's in.'

Still grumbling, Josh followed the two girls into the jungle beyond the fallen fence.

'If you have to pay for it, we'll help you out, won't we?' Holly said. 'Won't we, Amy?'

Amy bent down in the tall grass. 'Whoa!' she said, turning and showing them what she had picked up. 'Our ball!' she said. 'I didn't think we'd ever find it.'

Josh groaned. 'We weren't supposed to find it,' he said. 'That was the whole point.'

Amy shrugged and tossed the ball over her shoulder. 'There,' she said. 'It's lost again. Satisfied?'

'Let's take a look at the shed,' said Holly. 'That's what we're in here for. A quick look, then we can sort the fence out. Stop looking so miserable, Josh. It'll be OK.'

With a last despairing look at the ruined fence, Josh followed Holly and Amy as they waded through the grass towards the shed.

'Ouch!' said Amy. 'I've been stung! It's these rotten nettles. They're everywhere.'

'You should have worn jeans like me,' said Holly.

'I don't play tennis in jeans,' said Amy. 'Ow! Now I've scratched myself on a thorn. Oh, heck! And there are wasps! I hate wasps!' She waved her arms about. 'Shoo! Go away! Don't bite me, I taste horrible!'

'Wasps don't bite, they sting,' said Josh. 'And stop flapping about. You'll only annoy them.'

Holly reached the tumbledown shed and lifted the strut of wood away from the door. The door opened on its own on rusty hinges.

All manner of junk was piled inside. A broken old lawn-mower, paint tins, flowerpots, and heaps of other stuff, laced with cobwebs and coated with grime.

'Well?' said Josh as Holly ducked her head into the shed. 'See anything?'

'Just rubbish,' said Holly. Behind Josh, Amy was still windmilling her arms in an effort to keep the buzzing wasps at bay. Holly stepped cautiously into the shed. It was very gloomy inside, and smelt of mould and rot.

'What are we looking for?' Josh asked from the doorway.

'Anything to show someone's been in here recently,' said Holly, wiping a trail of spider's web off her shoulder. 'This place must be spider heaven,' she said. 'Everything's covered in webs.'

Josh shuddered. 'I don't think I want to go in there,' he said. 'I'm not very fond of spiders.'

Holly grinned back at him. 'You big softie,' she said. 'Spiders can't hurt you!'

'All the same ...' began Josh.

'Whoop!' yelled Amy, cannoning into Josh as a particulary ferocious wasp took a dive at her.

Josh found himself in the shed whether he liked it or not. Amy pulled the door shut behind them.

'That'll stop them,' she said. 'I think we'd better wait until they go away. I'm bound to get stung.'

With the door closed, it was almost pitch-black in the shed. The only light filtered in through cracks in the walls and roof.

'You clown!' said Holly. 'Open that door. I can't see what I'm doing.' *Crash!* Holly stumbled over something solid and fell.

'I'm not opening the door until those wasps have gone,' said Amy.

Holly's eyes gradually adjusted to the lack of light. She'd landed on something reasonably soft. She sat up, feeling under herself.

'It feels like cardboard,' she said, running her hand along a smooth edge. She blinked a couple of times, trying to see better.

'Is it the boxes?' asked Josh, trying not to think of spiders.

'Sort of,' said Holly. 'But they're flattened out. It's a whole pile of flattened-out boxes, I think.' As she felt about in the darkness, there was a sudden burst of light from the door.

'That's better,' she said. 'I can see now.'

'What in heaven's name do you three think you're playing at?' shouted a man's voice.

Holly snapped her head round.

This was the second time they'd been caught in mid-investigation. Holly groaned. This was becoming a habit!

6

Operation car-wash

'Oh! Hello, Dad,' said Josh. 'We … I – you see …'

'Out!' ordered Mr Hamilton. He was in his office suit. There was a thunderous expression on his face as the K.I.D.Z. trooped sheepishly out of the shed and lined up in front of him.

'You're home early,' said Josh. 'I wasn't expecting you for another couple of hours.' He gave his father a hopeful look. 'Did you have a good day?'

'Never mind all that,' Mr Hamilton said sternly. 'What are you doing over here, and what have you done to my fence?'

'We were playing tennis,' said Holly.

'And our ball went over the fence,' continued Amy.

'And when I tried to climb the fence,' added Holly, 'it sort of collapsed. I'm ever so sorry.' She gave him a weak smile. 'We'll fix it for you.'

'You were looking for your ball?' Mr Hamilton said slowly.

'That's right,' said Josh.

'In the shed?'

'Um …' began Josh.

'Wasps!' said Amy. 'We were hiding from wasps.' She looked round. The wasps had taken themselves off to another part of the garden. She pointed towards them. '*Those* wasps,' she said.

'I see,' said Mr Hamilton. Holly got the impression he wasn't entirely convinced. 'Come with me.'

They followed him back into Josh's garden.

'Josh,' he said. 'Go and fetch my toolbox.'

Josh went.

'I'm sure the fence can be mended,' said Holly.

Mr Hamilton shook his head. 'I can't leave you lot alone for five minutes, can I?' he said. '*Something* always happens when the three of you get together.'

Josh came running down the garden with his father's toolbox. It took them half an hour to get the section of fencing back in place and to hammer it home with a few well-placed nails.

They found out why Mr Hamilton was home early. He'd taken a couple of hours off with the intention of going to the second-hand shop in Croftleigh Road and picking up a DVD player.

With the fence mended, Holly and Amy were sent home, while Josh and his father got into their car for the trip to Square Deal to buy a DVD player.

'Do you think he was annoyed?' asked Amy as the two girls walked along together.

'Just a bit.' Holly sighed. 'I wonder if grown-up investigators have these problems?'

'What? Being caught hiding in sheds by their dads?' Amy said with a grin. 'I doubt it. Still, it's a pity there wasn't anything interesting in there. Apart from those folded-up old boxes.'

'They weren't folded-up *old* boxes,' said Holly. 'They were folded-up new boxes.'

'What makes you say that?' asked Amy.

'You saw the state of everything else in that shed,' said Holly. 'If that cardboard had been there any length of time, it would have gone rotten like everything else. They must have been put in there recently.'

'Oh. Right,' said Amy. 'So what do you make of that?'

'I don't know,' said Holly. 'But I intend to find out.'

Holly considered phoning Josh that evening, but thought better of it. She and Amy weren't exactly Mr Hamilton's favourite people just then. It would probably be wise, she decided, to give him time to cool off.

Amy had a late class to attend the following afternoon, so Holly met up with Josh on her own at the railway station as he got off the train home from his school.

'I'll be glad when I don't have to make that journey any more,' said Josh. 'It's been arranged for me to start at your school on Monday week.'

'Great,' said Holly. 'Our K.I.D.Z. work will be a lot easier with the three of us all together during the day as well as in the evenings.'

They headed off to Josh's house. Amy had arranged to meet them a little later, after her class.

All day, Holly had been trying to make sense of the information they had gathered.

What were the boxes for?

For putting things in.

But *what*? And *why*?

'Because they want to keep the stuff that was in the boxes secret,' said Josh as the two of them walked into his house. 'An empty house like that would be the perfect place to keep things hidden.'

'But what *sort* of things?' asked Holly.

'Guns?' Josh suggested. 'They could be international gunrunners. Or drugs?'

Holly looked unhappily at him. 'I hope it's neither of those,' she said. 'Especially not *guns*.'

'Don't worry,' said Josh. 'It won't be guns. Not in cardboard boxes. Guns would be too heavy. But I've been thinking about what you said before – about spies. Maybe the house *is* being used for surveillance. That would explain the camera.'

'And the boxes could be full of spying stuff, like I said,' added Holly. 'Do you really think so?'

'It could be private investigators,' said Josh.

'They could be watching people in another house over there. It could be a stake-out.'

'And that man who was pretending to be a meter reader is one of them,' said Holly. 'Oh! it drives me *mad*, not knowing what's going on over there!'

Josh opened his front door.

'We should write this all down when Amy gets here,' said Josh. 'I'm sure she'll have some ideas, too.'

'I bet she will,' said Holly. 'And they'll all be to do with terrible murders.'

'Do you want to see our new DVD?' said Josh. He led Holly into their sitting-room. The DVD player was set up next to the television.

Josh fumbled with the controls for five minutes but the television screen stayed just a mass of white interference.

'Do you know how to work it?' asked Holly.

'Of course I do,' said Josh. 'I'm brilliant at stuff like this. Just give me a minute.'

'Where are the instructions?' asked Holly.

'I don't know,' said Josh. He nodded across the room. 'Have a look in the box.' A cardboard box lay open on the floor. Holly rooted through the packaging debris, but there was no instruction manual.

'They did *give* you an instruction leaflet, didn't they?' asked Holly.

'Oh, I don't know,' Josh said in exasperation. 'I can't be bothered with this any more. That's the problem with buying second-hand stuff. Maybe there's something wrong with it. I expect Dad will be able to figure it out.'

It wasn't long before Amy arrived and the K.I.D.Z. went up to their office to talk things over.

'Theory number one,' said Holly, writing in her notebook. The page was headed *Case file: Midnight lights*. 'The house is being used by secret agents for surveillance.'

'When did you decide that?' asked Amy.

'We talked about it earlier,' said Josh. 'Before you got here.'

'You're not supposed to have ideas when I'm not here,' said Amy. 'We're supposed to discuss these things together.'

'I can't help having ideas,' said Holly. 'What am I supposed to do? Stop thinking when you're not around?'

'If you're putting *that* theory down,' Amy demanded. 'Then my idea about the murderer should go down as well.'

'What? Even though it doesn't fit in with anything we've found out?' said Josh.

'What exactly *have* we found out?' said Amy. 'For all we know, those boxes could have been full of stuff left by the previous owners.'

'So why move them in the middle of the night?' asked Josh. 'Your theory doesn't explain the flashlight from the camera, or the loose panel by the door, or that man pretending to want to read the electricity meter.'

'That's right,' said Holly. 'Those boxes are definitely the key to this whole mystery.'

'But they were *moved*,' Amy insisted. 'They probably aren't even in the house any more.' She paused. 'Oh! Except that Sparky turned up after the boxes had been moved.'

'Which means they must still be in the house somewhere,' said Josh. 'He came back to check that everything was OK.'

'But he *couldn't* check anything because we were in there,' said Holly. 'So he'll come back again, won't he?'

'He might already have been back,' said Amy.

'Surely it'd be worth us checking the place out again, just in case,' said Holly. The other two stared at her. She shook her head. 'I don't mean we try to get *in* there again. I mean we should come up with some plan where we can keep an eye on the house without drawing attention to ourselves. I *really* want to know what's going on in there.'

Josh sighed. 'I suppose you mean *I* should keep watch from my window.'

'No,' said Holly. 'We need to keep our eyes on the front of the house. I've had an idea.'

'Brilliant disguises?' said Amy. 'We dress up as three privet hedges and stand in the front garden?'

'Not exactly,' said Holly. 'Car-washing!'

'Car-washing?' chorused Josh and Amy.

Holly nodded. 'Our school has just started a fund-raising campaign for new computer terminals,' she told Josh. 'If we could get Mr Taylor to agree to us setting up a car-washing service, we could spend hours in Roseway Road without anyone suspecting anything. You never know, we might even find out who is being watched. And we'd be making money for the school. What do you say?'

Josh and Amy looked at each other.

'Can we do it in disguise?' asked Amy.

'No!' said Holly. 'No disguises.'

Amy sighed. 'I never get to wear any disguises,' she said. 'What's the fun in spying on people if you can't wear disguises?'

Mr Taylor was all in favour of Holly's scheme. After a lecture on not pestering people who didn't want their cars washed, and on doing a good and thorough job, he got the school secretary to type out a letter for the three friends. The letter stated that all monies collected would be used by the school. He also gave them a form to be signed by anyone who gave them money.

They got to work on Friday afternoon. Holly attached the form to a clipboard. Armed with a bucket, a bottle of all-purpose cleaner and several sponges and cloths, they made their way into Roseway Road.

There was no answer to Holly's ring at the first three houses.

'No one's in,' she complained. 'It's too early. Perhaps we should come back later?'

'Then everyone will be eating dinner or watching their favourite TV programme,' said Josh. 'Don't give up yet.'

Holly rang at another door. A harassed-looking young woman appeared with a baby in her arms and a small child clinging to her skirt.

'Hello,' said Holly in her politest voice. She went into her prepared speech while the other two waited at the gate.

The door slammed and she walked back down the short path.

'No luck?' asked Amy.

'No car!' said Holly.

At the next house they had more luck – or so they thought at first. The man who answered the door was delighted by their offer. Except that it wasn't a car he wanted washed. It was a huge motor-bike. It was parked on the concrete front under a grimy tarpaulin.

It was filthy. It looked as if it hadn't been used for years.

'Do a good job, mind,' said the man, after they had filled their bucket from his kitchen sink. 'I'm not paying up until it's spotless.'

It took the three of them over an hour to clean the motor-bike to his satisfaction. He even had them polishing the metalwork and rubbing at the leather seat until they could almost see their faces in it.

They did their best to keep an eye on the empty house.

'Look at me!' said Amy as they collected their money and came back out on to the pavement. 'I'm absolutely filthy! I'm fed up with this. And there hasn't been a sign of anyone going *near* that house. I'm going home!'

'Amy!' called Holly as her friend marched off down the road. 'Don't give up!'

'Too late,' Amy yelled back. 'I quit!'

Josh looked unhappily at Holly.

'It's OK,' she said. 'She'll come back once she's calmed down.'

But Amy didn't come back. Josh and Holly cleaned three cars before they gave up as well. It really was beginning to look as if they were wasting their time.

'Oh, well,' Holly said eventually. 'At least we made a bit of money for the school. Tomorrow's Saturday. I'll give Amy a call in the morning and we can have another meeting. Perhaps we'll be able to come up with another idea by then.'

The car-washing plan had proved to be a lot of hard work for nothing.

7

Boxes in, boxes out

Holly had only just got out of bed on Saturday morning when Amy appeared at the front door, dressed in an old T-shirt and torn jeans.

'Well?' she said. 'Are we washing cars today or not?'

'I thought you were sick of it,' said Holly.

'Yesterday I was. Today I'm not,' said Amy. 'Today I'm full of enthusiasm.'

Holly looked suspiciously at her. 'Why?'

Amy grinned. 'Mum's decided our house needs spring-cleaning,' she said. 'This was the only way I could get out of it.'

'It isn't spring,' said Holly.

Amy laughed. 'Try telling that to my mum,' she

said. 'Come on, slowcoach, let's go and root Josh out. I've got a feeling we're going to be lucky today.'

Josh was as surprised as Holly by Amy's change of heart, until he learned the reason.

'Is washing cars easier than spring-cleaning, then?' he asked as they walked down to Roseway Road with their equipment.

'It is when Mum's gone out and left Becky and Rachel in charge,' said Amy. Becky and Rachel were Amy's older twin sisters. 'I'd rather slave for us than slave for them,' said Amy.

They had much better luck this time. There were plenty of people in, and once they'd been told the money would be going to the local school, most people were more than happy to have the three friends wash their cars.

Holly's bum-bag was getting quite heavy with coins by lunch-time. The only disappointment was that in the three hours they'd been working, no one had gone into the empty house.

At midday they had a brief rest, sitting on a wall across the road from the house and a little way down the street. Josh handed chocolate bars round.

'If no one goes there today, do we have to come

back tomorrow?' asked Amy.

'We'll run out of cars to clean by then,' said Josh. 'In fact, if something doesn't happen pretty soon, we're going to be so far down the road we won't even be able to see the house any more.'

'Something will happen,' said Holly.

'Ha!' Amy mumbled through a chunk of chocolate.

All three of them were wet and grubby from their work. Half a bucket of soapy water had gone all over Amy's shoes and it was only the thought of being ordered about by her sisters that stopped her from squelching off home. Holly's arms were aching so much she hardly had the strength to wring out the cleaning cloth.

They were just about to ring at yet another door when a small van came cruising past. *Drip-Busters!* proclaimed the sign on the side. *Twenty-four-hour plumbers.*

The van came to a stop at the kerb outside the empty house and two men got out.

'Look!' squealed Amy.

'Don't *watch* them,' said Holly. 'Pretend we're busy.'

The three of them went back to polishing the

last car they had been working on. Something was finally happening!

The men were in overalls. One of them went round to open the back doors of the van, whilst the other headed up the path to the empty house's front door.

The man at the back of the van was wearing a baseball cap low over his eyes.

Holly tried to see what the other man was doing in the sunken doorway, but the trailing jasmine was in the way. When he came back down the path, she could see that the front door had been opened.

'Did you see him at that loose bit of glass?' hissed Josh. 'Was that how he got the door open, or did he have a key?'

'I couldn't see,' said Holly, peering over the bonnet of the car.

As the three friends watched, the men began ferrying boxes into the house.

'See the short one with the baseball cap?' said Josh. 'I've seen him somewhere before.'

'Keep down!' said Holly. 'Don't stare at them. Amy, look *busy*, will you? Don't let them see we're watching them.'

'I wish that cap wasn't shading his face so much,' said Josh. 'If I can just get one good look at him, I'm sure I'll remember where I've seen him before.'

For the next few minutes the two men busied themselves with carrying boxes into the house.

'If they're the people doing the surveillance,' said Amy, crouching down and rubbing at a hubcap while she peeped round the front bumper of the car, 'how come they're taking more stuff *in* there?'

'Maybe this is a whole new lot of surveillance gear,' said Josh. 'I bet that's what it is. They're probably bringing in even more sophisticated stuff.'

'I'd love to know for certain what's going on in there,' said Holly.

One of the men came out of the house and closed the back of the van before disappearing inside again.

Several minutes went past with no further sign of the men.

Holly stood up. 'What do you think they're doing in there?'

'Setting up their equipment,' said Josh. 'Holly,

write down the number plate of the van. If we're going to find out who these people are, we need all the information we can get.'

'I've already done it,' said Holly. She showed Josh the clipboard. She had written down the details of the van, and a brief description of the two men. 'I don't need you telling me how to collect evidence,' she said. 'I've even got the time they arrived.'

'I'm going over there for a quick look,' said Amy.

'Don't be daft,' said Holly. 'They're bound to come out and catch you.'

'So?' said Amy. 'I'll ask them if they want their van cleaned. They're not going to know we're watching them. We want to try and find out who they are, don't we?'

Amy walked across the road, her wet trainers squelching.

'Oh, no! Just listen to her!' Holly groaned as Amy started whistling innocently. 'She always does that when she's trying to be cunning.'

At the van, Amy turned and gave a quick thumbs-up sign and grinned at them.

She walked up the path of the empty house.

The door was open a couple of centimetres, but the glass panel was in its proper place. If the men had got in that way, they had covered their tracks well.

She reached towards the door. She had her speech all ready.

She hesitated as she saw the blurry shape of a man in the hall through the glass door-panels.

'One half now, the rest later,' she heard a man say.

The door opened from the inside.

The two men were in the hall, weighed down by boxes.

'Oh, hello,' said Amy. 'I just wondered if you'd like us to wash your van. We're—'

'No, we don't,' snapped the man at the door. He was a big man, with short greying hair and a face like a bulldog.

Amy looked for any sign of nervousness or alarm on the men's faces. Anything that would give her some proof that they were up to something secretive. But there was nothing, apart from the fact that they were both a bit sweaty and red-faced from their work.

'It's for a good cause,' said Amy.

'We don't need our van cleaned,' said the big man, stepping forwards so that Amy was forced to back down the path, the hanging jasmine catching in her hair as she did so.

'Our school's collecting for new computer stuff,' Amy said as she backed out on to the pavement.

The man looked over his shoulder. 'Gary,' he said, 'give the kid some money.'

Across the road, Holly and Josh were watching with bated breath. What did Amy think she was doing?

The man put the box down on the pavement and opened the back doors of the van. Amy hovered nearby while the two men loaded their boxes into the van.

'Here,' said the man called Gary. He put his hand in his overall pocket and took out some coins.

'Oh, we can't take it for *nothing*,' said Amy. 'We'd have to do something in exchange. If you don't want your van cleaned, maybe we could help you loading stuff?'

The big man gave her an angry frown. He grabbed her wrist, scooped the coins out of Gary's hand and put them in hers. 'Take the money,' he said. 'Take it and go and bother someone else. We're busy.'

'If you're *sure*,' said Amy.

'I'm sure,' said the big man. 'Scram!'

'OK,' said Amy. 'Thanks a lot.'

She ran over to where Holly and Josh were waiting.

'You nutcase,' hissed Josh. 'What was all that about?'

'I was trying to see what they had in those boxes,' whispered Amy.

'And?' asked Holly.

Amy shook her head. 'I couldn't see anything,' she said. 'But they gave me some money.' She opened her fist and showed them the coins. 'They just wanted to get rid of me.' She told them what she had heard the big man say. ' "One half now, the rest later." '

'They're looking over here,' whispered Holly. 'We'd better look as if we're doing something.'

They went to another house and rang the bell, doing their best not to look as if they were watching the two men.

The man who answered the door agreed to

pay them to wash his car. Josh went through to fill their bucket while the girls waited on the path.

'The one in the baseball cap is called Gary,' Amy told Holly. 'And if we want a code-name for the other one, I think we should call him Bruiser. He looks like a real thug.'

Holly nodded and wrote the two names down.

Over the next few minutes the two men ferried boxes out of the empty house and stacked them in the back of the van.

'I don't get it,' said Amy. 'Why did they take boxes in and then bring them straight out again?' A slosh of soapy water splashed down Amy's jeans. 'Josh! Be careful, I'm wet enough as it is!'

The men got into the cab of the van and drove off. As the van rumbled away the three friends stopped their work and looked at one another.

'Maybe they weren't the same boxes,' said Josh.

Holly shook her head. 'Didn't you notice anything odd?' she said. 'Didn't you notice that the boxes seemed a lot lighter when they took them in than when they brought them out?'

'That's right,' said Josh. 'They carried a couple

of boxes each on the way in, but only one on the way out.'

'Whoo!' breathed Amy. 'Empty boxes *in* and full boxes *out*! Holly, you're right. They weren't putting stuff in the house. They were taking stuff out!'

8

Stolen goods

'Are you washing that car, or just standing and looking at it?' The man whose car they were supposed to be cleaning was on his doorstep, hands on hips, frowning at them.

They got back to work.

A few minutes later, and with a couple more coins in Holly's bag, the K.I.D.Z. gathered on the corner of Roseway Road to decide what they should do next.

'Did you get a good look at the man in the baseball cap?' Josh asked Amy. 'Did you recognise him?'

'What, Gary?' said Amy. She shook her head.

'He wasn't the fake meter reader, then?' said Holly.

'No,' said Amy. 'I've never seen that Gary man before in my life.'

'Well, *I* have,' insisted Josh. 'I just wish I could remember where.'

'What do we do now?' asked Amy.

'The big man said they were taking half now and the rest later, didn't he?' said Holly. 'Which means that whatever they were up to, they're clearing out, right?'

'It looks like it,' said Josh. 'Rats! Now we'll never know!'

'But there's still stuff in the house,' said Holly.

'Hold on a minute,' said Josh. 'If you're thinking what I *think* you're thinking, you can forget it.'

Amy looked bemused. 'What do you think she's thinking?'

'I think she's thinking about going back in that house,' said Josh.

'It's our last chance of finding out what's been going on in there,' said Holly.

'Now look here,' said Amy. 'We tried the front and got caught. We tried the *back* and got caught. What next? Tunnelling up from underneath, or are you planning on us parachuting down the chimney out of an aeroplane?'

'In through the front again,' said Holly. 'That's the easiest way. And this time we go straight upstairs. *That's* where Josh saw the lights, so that's where the rest of the stuff will be. It won't take us more than two minutes.'

'But Bruiser said they were coming back for the rest,' said Amy. 'They'll catch us.'

'They will if we stand here arguing about it all afternoon,' said Holly. 'Look, they've only been gone ten minutes. They've got to get to wherever they're going, unload the stuff and get back again. We've got plenty of time.'

'Do you think they're up to something illegal?' asked Amy.

'It's certainly something they don't want anyone to know about,' said Josh. 'I'm with Holly. This is our only chance to find out.'

'If we get caught,' said Amy, '*you* can think up your own excuses, right? I'm going to plead insanity.'

Josh laughed. 'We'll back you up on *that* one,' he said.

Holly didn't say anything to her friends, but

her stomach was turning over anxiously as the three of them walked back to the house. But she knew that if they didn't act *now* then they would *never* solve the mystery. And an unsolved mystery would nag at her for the rest of her *life*!

She glanced round. The street was empty.

'OK,' she said firmly. 'Here goes.'

They bundled into the doorway. It took only a moment to edge the glass panel open and reach in to turn the lock.

Once inside, they closed the door and replaced the panel.

Amy shivered. 'This is a really bad idea,' she mumbled. 'We're going to get caught. I know we are.'

'No, we aren't,' said Holly. 'Trust me.'

Amy gave a hollow laugh.

'Come on,' said Josh. 'We haven't got time to argue about it now.'

Holly led the way upstairs. The bare stair treads creaked under their feet. Amy's groan of unease echoed eerily in the stairwell. The stairs went up to a long landing with four doors leading off it. All four doors were closed.

Holly opened the first door. The room was

quite bare. Josh pushed the second door open and they found themselves looking into a bathroom.

They tiptoed along the landing and Holly opened another door into an empty room. They looked at one another. There was only one door left now. Only one more room. Holly wondered whether her frantic heartbeats sounded as loud to the others as they did to her. *Thump-thump, thump-thump.*

She turned the handle and pushed the door open.

Josh let out a groan of exasperation.

There was nothing in the room.

'Well?' said Amy. 'Now what?'

'The stuff must be downstairs,' said Josh. 'We should have checked the ground floor first.'

'Now he tells us,' said Amy. She looked along the landing, as if hoping a fifth door might suddenly have appeared.

'Hey,' she said, glancing upwards. 'Look!' A square opening was set into the ceiling above their heads.

'That just leads up into the roof space,' said Josh. 'You'd need a ladder to get up there.'

'So let's look for a ladder,' said Holly.

'Don't be daft,' said Josh. 'If those men had the

stuff up there, the ladder would be here, wouldn't it?' He headed for the stairs. 'I'm going to look downstairs.'

'Wait!' said Amy.

'Come on,' Josh said as he ran down the stairs. 'We're running out of time.'

'Coming?' Holly asked Amy. Every second that passed was making her more uneasy. She wanted to get out of the house as quickly as possible, whether they found anything or not.

'Just hold on a second,' said Amy. She had spotted something. A long pole resting in the corner. A pole with a metal hook on the end. She picked it up and looked again at the trap-door in the ceiling.

'Got it!' she said. 'See that ring?' Holly looked. There was a metal ring at one side of the trap-door. 'This hook goes into the ring so you can push the thing open,' said Amy. 'Watch.'

It took her a couple of attempts before she got the long pole under control and managed to slip the hook into the ring. She gave a hefty shove. The trap-door didn't move.

'Oh!' she said. 'I was *sure*—'

'Don't push it,' said Holly. 'Pull it. Why are you

always so useless with things like that? It opens downwards.' She took hold of the pole alongside Amy and they both gave a good hard tug. The trap-door grated open and the feet of a metal ladder slid out of the gap.

'Wow!' gasped Amy. 'A ladder! Come on, Holly. Pull!'

They forced the trap-door wider and the ladder edged down through the hole.

'There must be some kind of machinery up there,' said Holly. 'Attached to the door, so the ladder slides out when you open it. Give me the pole. It must pull right down.'

'I can do it,' said Amy.

'Don't argue,' said Holly, trying to get the pole out of Amy's hands. 'You'll do it all wrong.'

'Get off!' said Amy. 'I found it!' She elbowed Holly out of the way.

'Amy!' exclaimed Holly. 'Don't be so childish!' She made another lunge for the pole. 'We can do it together.'

But the hook on the end of the pole was still caught in the ring. The two of them fought to get it free. There was a sudden, sharp noise and the pole came free.

'Oh, brilliant!' said Amy. 'Now look what you've done!' The hook had come off the end of the pole and was dangling uselessly in the ring.

'Don't blame me,' said Holly. 'You were the one fighting to do it by yourself. I said you'd mess it up, didn't I?'

With a snort of annoyance, Amy yanked the pole out of Holly's hands and made a few attempts to jerk the ladder down.

'You'll never do it like that,' said Holly. She jumped up at the legs of the ladder. Her fingertips just scraped the foot. It was just out of reach.

'Josh's taller than us,' said Amy. 'He'll be able to reach it.'

'Wait,' said Holly. 'If you support me, I can climb up on the banister rail.' The banister ran the length of the landing, preventing a fall into the stairwell.

'Are you sure?' asked Amy.

'Of course I'm sure,' said Holly. 'But hurry!'

Amy made her hands into a stirrup. Holly took a firm grip of Amy's shoulder and lifted herself. She got one foot on top of the banister rail, her hand pressing down on Amy's head as she boosted herself into the air. Amy sagged under the weight.

For a second Holly teetered perilously in the air, trying to find her balance. She grabbed at the ladder and it came screeching down with the teeth-grating sound of metal on metal.

The two girls tumbled to the floor as the ladder thudded down beside them.

'Ha!' Holly laughed, springing to her feet. 'Got it!'

Amy sat up. 'You never do anything the easy way, do you?' she said.

Holly took no notice. She climbed the ladder.

Amy stood up and held the bottom of the ladder as she saw her friend's upper half disappear into the dark hole.

'Well?' she called up. 'Anything?'

'Wow!'

'What?' Amy climbed the ladder. '*What?*'

Holly clambered into the roof space. It was dark in there, but enough light filtered in through a filthy skylight for her to see. And what she saw, as she crouched on the floor up there, brought another 'Wow!' from her.

'What have you found?' asked Amy. Her head

came up into the roof space. 'Wow!' she breathed. 'Aladdin's Cave!'

It hadn't taken Josh more than a few seconds to check the ground-floor rooms. He checked the front room that Holly had seen through the bay window the other day and the back room with the French windows where they had first seen the boxes. Both were empty.

He ran down the three steps into the back kitchen. There was an old sink unit under a window and a couple of empty cupboards. But still no sign of any cardboard boxes.

It didn't make sense. Amy had said she'd heard one of the men say they were coming back for the rest of their stuff. But where *was* the rest?

Had Amy not heard correctly? Had the men decided to take everything in one go after all? Where *was* it?

He came out of the kitchen, baffled and frustrated. A door faced him. He hadn't spotted it on his way into the kitchen. A door under the stairs. It might just be a cupboard. On the other hand …

He opened the door. Steps led down into darkness. It was a cellar.

Josh grinned. That had to be it! Of course! The stuff would have been put somewhere safe. It wouldn't just be left lying around for anyone to find.

He pushed the door back against the wall. He tried the light switch, shaking his head at his own stupidity as the light failed to come on.

The electricity would have been turned off ages ago. He already *knew* that, but at least the girls weren't there to make fun of his silly action.

I'll just have to risk it in the dark, he thought.

He paused, every sense terribly alert as he heard a sound from the front of the house. The ominous sound of a large vehicle drawing up at the kerb.

Josh ran to the front door, his heart in his mouth, and peered through the glass.

The van was back.

9

Hide and seek

Even as Josh ducked down out of sight, two men were getting out of the cab of the van. The big man was there, but he didn't have Gary with him this time. The other man with him was Sparky. Josh recognised him immediately. So the fake meter reader *was* involved.

Josh hesitated long enough to see them go round to the back of the van and open the doors.

He ran to the foot of the stairs.

'Holly!' He tried to project his voice up the stairs in a frantic whisper. 'Amy! They're *back*! Quick!'

There was no answer. All he heard was a loud, metallic grating noise and a heavy thud. What were they *doing* up there?

He glanced round at the door. Through the frosted glass he could see the blurry shapes of the men coming up the path. There was no time for the girls to get down here even if they had heard him. They'd be caught on the stairs. And *then* what would happen?

Josh's brain raced. There was nothing upstairs – they'd already made sure of that. Holly and Amy were bound to hear the men come into the house. If they had any sense, they'd keep quiet as mice up there and wait until the men finished what they were doing and went away again.

Or would they? Josh hesitated for a moment, then went haring up the stairs to warn the two girls.

'Look at all this!' said Holly. Dust drifted in the air up into the roof space. The bare floor beams had been covered with plywood, and heaped all around the trap-door was a curious collection of things. There were DVD players and dismantled hi-fi units and cameras. There were piles of compact discs and handbags and wallets and jewellery boxes. There were silver ornaments and clocks. It was as if all the valuables from a dozen or more houses had been stashed away up here. There were even a couple of small portable televisions, trailing their wires across the floor.

Amy had been right – it *was* like Aladdin's Cave up here. A criminal Aladdin's Cave.

'This isn't surveillance stuff,' said Holly. 'It looks like *stolen* stuff.' She stared at Amy. 'They aren't using this place for *watching* anything – they're using it to stash stolen things.'

'The burglaries!' Amy gasped. 'Remember that man from next door said there had been a lot of burglaries in the area? Holly – what on earth have we got ourselves into?'

'We've got to call the police,' said Holly. 'Quickly! Before they come back.'

Amy pulled a tissue out of her pocket and held it to her face, trying to keep the dust from making her sneeze.

'They must have been burgling away like maniacs to get all this lot!' said Holly. 'There must be a *fortune* up here.'

'Don't just sit there looking at it,' said Amy. 'We've got to get out of here.'

'Hoy!' It was a sharp hiss from beneath them. Amy looked down and saw Josh's frightened face. 'They're *back*!'

'They're criminals!' said Amy. 'The attic is full of stolen stuff!'

'*What?*' Josh gasped in horror.

'They're burglars!' called Holly.

'Get down out of there,' panted Josh. 'We've got to hide.'

'Right,' said Holly. 'I'm coming. Out of the way.'

She crawled to the trap-door. Amy climbed down the ladder. As her foot touched the floor she heard the front door open beneath her.

'Get a move on!' she whispered up to Holly.

Holly's frightened face stared down at her through the hole. 'Hide! I'm coming.'

Josh grabbed Amy's arm.

'In here,' he said, dragging her towards the bathroom door. 'Holly, quick!'

As Josh hauled her through the bathroom door, Amy glanced back. She could see Holly's foot coming down through the hole. Would she get down in time?

In her panic to get out of the roof space, Holly

caught her jeans on the top of the ladder. She tugged wildly, trying to free herself, but a sharp edge of the ladder had snagged right through her jeans leg. The more she struggled to free herself, the worse it got.

With a soft yelp of despair, she lifted herself back up into the roof space. Above the hammering of her heart, she could hear the voices of the men coming up the stairs.

Over to one side, where the slope of the roof met the plywood flooring, was a thick roll of something. Not carpet – some kind of thick insulation material. Holly scampered over to it and stretched herself out behind it.

She forced herself to lie perfectly still. As long as the men didn't actually look over there, she had a chance of remaining hidden until they went away.

As she lay there listening to the throbbing of her heart, she hoped that Amy and Josh had managed to get themselves hidden away safely.

Holly Adams, she thought to herself, *you are the stupidest person in the entire world! You and your mysteries! Look at the mess you're in now!*

Amy and Josh crouched behind the bathroom door, straining to hear. Amy spotted the catch by the handle and silently slid it closed.

'Come on,' she heard one of the men say. 'We haven't got all day.' She recognised the voice. It was Bruiser.

'I thought I heard something,' came another man's voice from further away.

'Mice,' said Bruiser. 'Get up here.' He was on the landing now, horribly close to the door behind which Amy was crouching in terror.

'That fool,' she heard Bruiser say. 'I told Gary to put the ladder up.' He had obviously seen that the trap-door was open and that the ladder was down. 'He's going to get us all caught. What if that estate agent woman had brought someone here? I should wring his neck!'

That would be handy, thought Amy. *That would be one less burglar to deal with, at least.* She gave Josh an anxious look. Josh looked as scared as she felt.

'You know what he's like,' said the second man, his voice much closer now. Amy recognised

Sparky's voice.

'Yes,' snarled Bruiser. 'Useless!'

'Forget it,' said Sparky. 'No one's been here, and we'll have all the stuff out of here in ten minutes. You worry too much.'

'We're going to need some more boxes,' said Bruiser. Josh and Amy heard the metallic creak of the ladder as he stepped on the first rung. 'Where did Gary put them?'

'In the shed out back,' said Sparky.

'What? Why?' Bruiser sounded exasperated. 'Why did he put them out there?'

'You told him to hide them,' said Sparky. 'And they wouldn't go through the trapdoor. Do you want me to go and fetch them?'

'No. Leave it. We'll see how we get on with what we've got,' said Bruiser. 'We don't want to risk being seen in the garden unless we have to. Gary's a bigger idiot than you. I should have just strangled him then and there the other night when he set off that camera! I'm surrounded by fools!' The ladder creaked as he climbed. 'I'm going to beat Gary's brains out when we get back to the shop,' he said. 'I knew we couldn't rely on him.'

They heard Sparky laugh. 'What brains?' he said.

That explains the flash of light, thought Josh. *One of them set a flashbulb off by accident.*

Bruiser said something that they didn't catch. Judging by the tone of his voice, Amy felt quite glad she hadn't heard properly. It didn't sound particularly polite.

Bruiser's voice echoed from further away. *He must be up in the roof space now.* Amy looked at Josh and crossed her fingers. He nodded. Their only hope was that Holly was well hidden up there. All this talk of necks being wrung and brains being beaten out was very alarming.

Holly held her breath, trying to flatten herself against the floor. Trying to make herself as small as possible behind the roll of material.

Please don't look this way, she prayed.

She heard a man scrabbling about only a few metres from where she was hiding.

'Ready?' she heard him call down.

A second voice drifted up. 'Yes. Start handing

it down.'

There were grunts and scrapings as the man lowered things down for his partner on the ladder to take.

'Shall I fill the boxes as we go?' called the second man.

'No, let's get it all down out of here first.'

It seemed like a lifetime to Holly as she listened to the two men heaving the stolen stuff down from the attic. But at least there was one crumb of comfort – Amy and Josh hadn't been discovered. Maybe they would be able to get out of the house and phone the police.

'OK,' said the first man. 'Just the small stuff now.'

'Are we taking the jewellery and stuff to Gary's place?' asked the second man.

'Don't be stupid,' said the first man. 'Gary just gets the electrical stuff. All the rest is going off to a man I know. He'll give us cash.'

She heard a final grunt and groan from the man. 'That's the lot,' he said. 'Gah! My back!'

'You're getting old!' laughed the second man.

'Watch it! I'm not too old to teach you a lesson or two. I'll just—' The man's voice came to an abrupt halt. Holly heard the hiss of his breath. *Clump! Clump! Clump!* In three long strides the man covered the gap between the trap-door and Holly's hiding-place.

Holly let out a stifled yell as a rough hand grabbed her collar and she was dragged out into the open.

'What is it?' yelled the other man.

Blazingly angry eyes bored into Holly as she struggled hopelessly in the man's powerful grip.

'Get up here,' he yelled. He gave Holly a ferocious shake. 'We've got trouble!'

10

Trouble with a capital T

Amy and Josh could hear every word the men spoke from their hiding-place behind the bathroom door. They heard Bruiser call down, 'That's the lot.'

Josh grabbed Amy's arm, making her jump.

He put his mouth close to her ear.

'We're OK,' he whispered. 'They haven't found her.'

Amy nodded. A few minutes more and the men would leave the house. They'd be safe!

She uncrossed her fingers and let out a sigh of relief. The sigh turned into a gasp of misery as the man on the landing yelled suddenly and she heard scuffling noises from above her.

Josh's fingers dug into her arm.

There was no doubt about what had happened up there. Holly had been caught!

'We've got to help her,' whispered Josh.

'How?' breathed Amy. What could they do? If they were discovered, it wouldn't take those men ten seconds to overpower them. And then what might happen? Amy didn't even want to think about it.

Josh stared round the room. There was a pedestal basin, a bath, a toilet and a small wall cupboard. There was nothing in there that they could possibly use to try and rescue Holly.

But there was a way for them to escape. A small frosted-glass window above the toilet cistern.

Amy pointed to it.

Josh nodded, bringing his mouth close to her ear again. 'You get out,' he whispered. 'Call the police.'

'What about you?' said Amy.

'I'll think of something,' said Josh. 'I'll try and delay them.'

Amy crept across the floor. She climbed on

to the toilet cistern, jerking at the handle of the window. It was stiff, but panic lent her strength, and, after a few hefty yanks, the handle turned and she was able to shove the window open.

She looked round at Josh. He was standing by the door, his face white.

'Good luck,' he mouthed at her. 'Be *careful!*'

She leaned out of the window, forcing her shoulders into the narrow gap. The side wall fell a clear four metres down to the garden. Too far to jump, even if she could get herself feet first through the window.

But a thick black pipe was anchored to the wall only a few centimetres to the right of the window. If she could somehow haul herself out of the window, maybe she could shin down the pipe.

Using every ounce of her strength, Amy edged herself out through the window, twisting to catch hold of the pipe. She swivelled her hips, sat on the narrow sill and tried to draw her legs up to give herself some base from which she could swing out on to the pipe.

Her swinging foot caught on the flushing lever at the side of the cistern and she almost fell head first as the lever gave way beneath her. There was a rush of water as the toilet flushed.

She gathered herself together, and, silently praying that the pipe would hold, brought her feet up under her on the sill and swung out into empty air.

'Let go of me!' shouted Holly, twisting in Bruiser's grip, her legs kicking as he held her in the air. 'Let me *go!*'

He released her and she crashed to the floor.

She sat up, winded but unhurt. The powerful man stood over her. The head and shoulders of the second man – Sparky – appeared through the trap-door.

'It's one of those kids!' he gasped, his eyes round with amazement. 'They were in here a few days ago. With that estate agent woman.'

'Is that a fact?' growled Bruiser. 'And they were hanging about outside earlier as well.' He crouched over Holly, his angry face only centimetres from hers. 'Where are the others?'

'What others?' said Holly.

He caught hold of her shoulder and shook her roughly.

'Don't play games with me,' he snarled. 'There were three of you. The big-mouthed blonde girl and that weasel-faced boy. Where are they?' His eyes swivelled round the roof space, looking for the others. His eyes fixed on a huge water tank. 'Aha!'

'They're not here,' said Holly.

'Is that so?' said Bruiser. He let go of her and pounced towards the tank. 'I've got you!' he shouted. 'Come on out!' He gave a growl of annoyance as he saw that there was no one hidden there.

'What are we going to do?' shouted Sparky.

The big man came back to where Holly was sitting.

'Get up,' he said.

Holly scrambled to her feet, hoping that her shaking legs wouldn't collapse under her. She was determined not to show just how frightened she was.

'My friends aren't here,' she said steadily. 'They went to call the police. They'll be here any moment.'

Sparky gave a yell and vanished.

'Wait!' bellowed Bruiser.

'I'm getting out of here,' came Sparky's voice from below them. 'I'm not hanging around to be caught!'

'Idiot!' shouted Bruiser. 'They haven't called the police. She wouldn't be up here if they'd called the police. The other kids are in this house somewhere. Find them!'

'You find them!' Sparky yelled from the landing.

'Stop where you are!' shouted Bruiser. 'I'm coming down.' She pushed Holly ahead of him. She climbed down the ladder. Sparky was standing at the head of the stairs. Holly thought that he looked even more scared than her.

Bruiser descended, his hand locking on Holly's shoulder again as he glared at Sparky.

'Search every room,' he said. 'Get those kids!'

'But the *police*,' moaned Sparky.

'Shut up about the police,' said Bruiser. 'Are you thick, or what? She wouldn't have been hiding up there if they'd called the police. They're just nosing around on the off-chance.'

'Oh, yes?' exclaimed Holly. 'So how come

we know what you've been up to? We've been watching this place for days. We know *everything*.'

The big man's grip was like a vice on her shoulder. 'Is that a fact?' he growled. He looked at his accomplice. 'Don't just stand there! Search!'

Sparky hesitated for a moment, as if torn between bolting down the stairs and obeying the big man. Then he ran to the first room, sending the door crashing open.

He ran out again and hurled himself at the second door.

Holly held her breath as Sparky twisted the handle on the bathroom door and crashed face first against it as it failed to open. Amy and Josh had locked it from inside, Holly realised. But how long would the door stay closed against two strong men?

Sparky reeled back, clutching his nose and howling. He'd hit that door with plenty of force.

'Kick it in!' shouted Bruiser.

'I've busted my nose!' yelled Sparky.

'You clown,' growled Bruiser. 'Hold her! I'll do it!'

As the big man braced himself to give the locked bathroom door a shoulder-charge, the most unexpected sound in the world came from the room beyond.

The distinct sound of a toilet flushing.

'Stop!' It was Josh's voice from beyond the door, shouting frantically. 'I'm coming out!'

Bruiser gave Holly a nasty smile. 'So they've gone for the police, have they?' he said. He rattled the door handle and hammered on the door. 'Get out here,' he shouted.

'I'm trying,' came Josh's voice from within the bathroom. 'The lock's stuck.'

Bruiser growled. Holly could tell from his expression that he wasn't just going to stand around waiting while Josh fiddled with the lock.

Holly's mind raced. Sparky was holding her by one arm, and she could feel that he was shaking. She was certain that the lock wasn't really stuck. This was her best chance to escape, while the big man was being distracted by Josh.

Bruiser backed away from the door and charged with one hefty shoulder lowered. The door opened a split second before he hit it, catching him off-balance. Holly heard a cry from Josh as the door crashed open and the big man went careering into the room.

Holly gulped in a huge breath and let out a piercing scream. Sparky jumped with surprise, his fingers loosening on her arm as she twisted herself free and leaped for the stairs.

Josh was almost knocked off his feet as the door came smashing open under Bruiser's charge. The big man staggered, falling as he burst into the room, his hands grabbing for Josh.

But Josh was too quick for him. He ran out into the hallway just as Holly let out her scream and got free of Sparky.

'Run!' he yelled to Holly. But Holly was already ahead of him, bounding down the stairs.

Josh leaped after her, but was brought to a halt as a hand grabbed his collar and tipped him over backwards on the stairs.

It had taken Sparky only a moment to recover from the shock of Holly's escape. He pulled Josh down and dived towards Holly, his fingers clawing at her fleeing back.

Holly let out a cry as she felt a jerk on her hair.

'Got you!' yelled Sparky.

Holly was almost at the foot of the stairs. Clinging on to the banister rail, she twisted her head, trying to pull free.

Holly didn't see exactly what happened next, but Josh did. As he pulled himself to his feet, he saw Sparky trip on the stairs and fall forwards past Holly and into the hallway.

Then Bruiser came blundering out of the bathroom and Josh leaped down the stairs. Sparky was just getting to his feet – and now he was between them and the front door.

'This way!' Holly yelled, spinning round the banister rail. With Sparky between them and the front of the house, their only hope of escape was out through the back.

Josh raced after Holly as she headed alongside the stairs.

They dashed into the kitchen and Holly struggled briefly with the handle of the back door. But it wouldn't budge.

Bruiser's feet thundered on the stairs, and as Holly and Josh looked round, they saw Sparky at the kitchen door, his face twisted with anger.

'Josh! The window!' yelled Holly.

Josh's head snapped round. The window was over the sink unit. He jumped up on to the top of the unit and grabbed for the handle. It wasn't locked, but he wasn't prepared for how easily the window sprang open. With a cry, he fell head first through the window and landed, sprawling, in the garden.

Holly was only a second behind him. She heard Sparky give a yell and saw him spring towards her out of the corner of her eye. She hurled herself on to the sink unit, but Sparky was too quick for her. A hand closed round her ankle and jerked her backwards.

She struggled, feeling the unit come away from the wall. The sink unit wasn't built to withstand this sort of pressure. The water pipes ruptured and sent a blast of water into Sparky's face. For a split second, he floundered against the powerful gush of water. Then he fell.

The water fountained into the air from the broken pipe. Holly also crashed to the ground, her feet sliding on the flooded floor.

Sparky lay quite still as the water swirled round him. But even as Holly scrambled to her feet, Bruiser came bursting into the room. He took one look at the chaos and let out a bellow of rage.

Holly dived for the open window. But she was too late. A strong arm caught her and dragged her backwards out into the hallway.

'You're coming with me,' Bruiser snarled as he half-carried her along the hallway towards the front door. 'No one's going to try and stop me while I've got you as a hostage!'

11

Holly in trouble

As Amy edged her way down the pipe, she heard a crash from within the room. The men had broken in – Josh was caught! She lost her grip and fell with a brief scream down to the ground.

She fell about two metres into an overgrown flower-bed that lay against the wall. Feathery seeds billowed up around her as she scrambled to her feet. She had landed well, but as she made a dash for safety, one of her feet caught on some hidden wire and she was sent sprawling on her face.

For a few agonising seconds she tried to untangle her shoe from the clutching wire. With a scream of frustration, she kicked the shoe off and staggered to her feet. The garden fence was only six metres away. Once over that she would be in Josh's garden, and only a sprint away from the telephone. *If* she made it. And if she could get *into* Josh's house!

She ploughed through the tall grass.

'What in heaven's name is going on over there?' she heard.

She spun round. A familiar old face stared at her over the side fence. An angry face under a floppy old fishing-hat. It was Mr Frazer, the bad-tempered next-door neighbour.

'You again!' he shouted. 'I might have known!'

'Help!' yelled Amy. 'Burglars! My friends! In there!' She was out of breath and frantic with panic. It was hardly surprising that she didn't make much sense as she blundered through the grass towards the side fence.

'Help?' shouted the old man. 'I'll give you *help!* I'm going to call the police this time. *That's* what I'm going to do!'

'Good!' yelled Amy. 'Do it! Do it *now!*'

She hardly knew where she got the strength from. As the astonished old man backed away, she made a flying leap over the fence and landed in his garden.

'Phone the police!' Amy screamed. 'Quick! Before they get away!'

Mr Frazer stared at her in disbelief as she rushed past him towards the house.

'Now, look here,' he shouted, chasing her in through the open back door.

An old woman sat at the kitchen table, peeling potatoes.

'Where's your phone?' yelled Amy. 'Quickly, please! I've got to call the police!'

'It's in the hall,' said the woman. 'But—'

'Thanks.'

Mr Frazer came to a halt in the hall as he heard Amy gabbling into the telephone.

'What's going on?' he puffed. 'Will you please explain—'

Amy slammed the phone down. 'No time,' she panted. 'I've got to get back.'

She almost knocked Mr Frazer flying as she pelted out through the house. No way was she going to leave Holly and Josh in there with those men!

She gave no thought to her aches and bruises as she dragged herself back over the garden fence.

Even as she bounced down into the garden, she

saw Josh getting to his feet after his fall from the kitchen window.

'Josh!' she yelled. 'Where's Holly?'

Josh turned to look in through the open window. Water was still gushing from the broken pipes and Sparky was lying motionless under the cascade. But there was no sign of Holly.

'She's gone!' he cried. 'She was right behind me with Bruiser.'

The slamming of the front door echoed through the house.

Josh stared at Amy in dismay. 'He must have caught her!' He heaved himself up on to the window-sill and jumped through the window, skidding and sliding as he sprinted across the kitchen floor.

He was in the hallway in a moment, dashing towards the front door. He jerked it open just in time to see the van pulling away from the kerb.

'Stop!' he yelled as he ran out on to the pavement. 'Somebody stop him!'

But there was no one to hear his shouts. The van gathered speed and swept away down the road.

Holly was in the passenger seat, clinging on for dear life as the big man drove recklessly along the road, spinning the wheel to make one screeching turn after another.

She glanced at the handle on the passenger door. She was no coward, but she knew it would be foolish to try and escape with the van going at such a speed.

'Where are you taking me?' she gasped as Bruiser's wild driving flung her from side to side.

'Shut up!' A heavy hand came out, pushing her down on to her side on the wide seat. 'Keep your head down and keep your mouth shut!'

She could no longer see where they were going. All she was aware of was the violent rattling of the van, and the stomach-turning swerves as they raced through the streets. Then a few minutes later the van came to a sudden halt, its brakes screaming.

The engine cut out. In the sudden quiet Holly could hear the panting of Bruiser's breath. She lifted her head. They had stopped in a narrow cul-de-sac. Brick walls reared all round her.

'Come on,' said Bruiser, shoving the driver's door open and catching hold of her collar.

It was all Holly could do to keep on her feet as he pulled her out of the van and dragged her towards a doorway set into the side wall.

'Let me go!' she gasped. 'You're hurting me!'

But Bruiser's grip was as hard as ever as he pushed the door open and thrust her through.

The door slammed behind them. They were in some kind of storeroom. Heavy metal shelves were filled with all kinds of electrical goods, and there were boxes piled everywhere.

'Keep quiet and you won't come to any harm,' said Bruiser. 'One word out of you and you'll be sorry.'

Holly nodded, swallowing hard.

I'll be all right, she said to herself. *Josh and Amy will call the police.* But what help would *that* be? How long would it take them to find out where Bruiser had taken her?

Holly preferred not to think about that.

Bruiser led her to another doorway. He listened for a moment before opening the door a fraction.

'Gary!' he called. 'In here!'

The man called Gary came through.

'That was quick,' he began. 'You can put the stuff …' His voice trailed off as he saw Holly.

'I need some money,' said Bruiser.

'Who's *she*?' gasped Gary. He stared at Bruiser. 'What's going *on*?'

'We caught her nosing about in the house,' said Bruiser. 'Her and some other kids.'

'Where's Grant?' asked Gary.

'I don't know, and I don't care,' growled Bruiser. 'We've had it, you fool! The other kids will call the police. I'm going to get as far away from here as I can. And she's coming with me. The police won't try and stop me if they know I've got her on board.'

Holly saw the panic in Gary's face. 'What about *me*?' he gasped. 'They'll trace the stuff here.'

'That's your problem,' snarled Bruiser. 'Money! Now!'

'I – I'll get it from the till,' stammered Gary. He gave Holly a final frantic glance as he ran from the room.

'Where are you going to take me?' asked Holly, her brain racing. But Bruiser remained silent.

The door burst open and Gary came back in.

He had a wad of bank-notes in his hand.

'This is all I could find,' he said. 'Let's get out of here.'

Bruiser snatched the money out of his hand. 'You're not coming with me,' he said.

'You've got to take me!' cried Gary. 'You can't just leave me.' He snatched at Bruiser's arm, but the big man shook him off.

'No way!' he said, pulling Holly towards the back entrance.

Gary let out a shout and jumped at the big man. With an angry grunt, Bruiser elbowed him away. Gary stumbled over backwards, crashing into a stack of cardboard boxes.

Now! thought Holly. She twisted in Bruiser's grip and felt his fingers slip away from her collar.

She ran to the door and caught hold of the handle. But Bruiser was on her in a second. His hand closed round her wrist and he wrenched the door open.

'No more tricks,' he growled. 'Get in the van.'

Her heart beating fast and her legs shaking, Holly climbed into the van. Escape now seemed impossible.

Two police cars came roaring up to the empty house on Roseway Road. No more than five minutes had elapsed since Amy's phone call. Old Mr Frazer was out on the pavement with Josh and Amy. They had done their best to explain to him what had happened, but they were both too panicky for anything they said to make much sense.

Amy ran forwards as the police officers got out of the cars.

'They've taken our friend!' she shouted. 'You've got to do something! They've taken her off in the van.'

'Calm down,' said one of the officers, taking Amy by the shoulders. 'Tell me exactly what's happened. Did you disturb burglars?'

'Yes! No!' babbled Amy. 'They weren't burglars – I mean, they *were* burglars, but they weren't—'

'This place is full of stolen stuff,' interrupted Josh. 'And there's one of them in there.' He pointed towards the open front door. 'I think he's unconscious. But the other one has taken Holly.

In a van. A blue van with "Drip-Busters!" written on the side. They were pretending to be plumbers. Amy? What was the number of the van?'

'I don't remember,' wailed Amy. 'Holly had it written down.'

'Go and check in there,' said the police officer to the others. He looked at Mr Frazer. 'Can you tell me what happened?'

'He doesn't know anything,' said Amy. 'Please! You've got to get after the van.'

The officer spoke into his shoulder transmitter. 'We're at the scene,' he said. 'I'm not sure what's happened, but it looks like a girl has been taken hostage.' He gave Josh's description of the van. A voice crackled back.

'OK,' said the police officer. 'I'll get all the details I can from this end.'

'We've told you everything!' said Amy.

'He's unconscious, all right,' shouted a policeman from the doorway of the house. 'There's water everywhere. It looks like there's been a real battle in here.'

'How many men were there?' asked the first officer. 'Could you describe them?'

'There were three of them,' said Josh.

'*Two*,' said Amy. 'A big, grey-haired man and a younger one with dark-brown hair. They were wearing overalls – grey overalls.'

'There were three altogether,' said Josh. 'The third one was called Gary – but he wasn't with them the second time.'

The police officer stared at him. 'The *second* time?' he said. 'What do you mean?'

'There isn't time to explain,' said Josh. 'But there *were* three of them, and – *oh*!' His face suddenly lit up. 'I've got it!' He grabbed Amy's arm. 'I've *got* it! I know where I've seen that man before! I just remembered!'

12

You can't win them all

Holly squeezed herself into the corner of the seat, trying to keep as far away from Bruiser as possible. He slammed the van door closed and started the engine. Things were happening so fast, she could hardly think.

The big man was sweating heavily as he jerked at the gear lever and swung the wheel. The van jumped forwards and there was a loud bang as the front bumper hit the wall of the narrow alley. Holly was thrown forwards.

With a snarl, Bruiser wrenched the gear lever back and turned the wheel again, sending the van careering backwards. There was another bang and a scraping noise as the rear of the van collided with the other wall.

Holly could see the panic on his face. At this rate the van would be wrecked before he got it out of the alley.

He muttered a curse and shoved the door open, leaning out to see what damage had been done in his frantic efforts to drive clear.

Holly looked at the ignition keys dangling from the steering block. She only had a second to act. She snatched at the keys and twisted them out of the ignition. She yanked the door handle down with her other hand and threw her full weight against the door. She tumbled out of the van, scrambled to her feet and ran.

The mouth of the alley was only a few metres away. Holly came pelting out into the street, gasping for breath. She recognised the street immediately. The row of shops. The empty area where the Sunday street market was held.

She was in Croftleigh Road. And the shop that stood alongside the alley was the second-hand shop where Josh had bought his DVD!

She ran out into the road and screamed at the top of her voice.

'Help!'

People in the street turned to stare at her and a couple of people ran towards her. Bruiser was at the mouth of the alley, looking like a wild animal at bay as he saw the people running towards Holly.

Before Holly had time to gather her breath again, the whooping of police sirens filled the air. A police car came hurtling round the corner, screeching to a halt only a couple of metres from where she was standing.

She let out a yell of joy as she saw Bruiser turn and run.

But he didn't get far. Two police officers ran after him into the alley and brought him down.

A third policeman ran over to Holly.

'It's OK,' he said. 'You're safe now.'

'What about the others?' said Holly. 'Are *they* all right?'

A second police car rounded the corner and stopped behind the first one.

A back door burst open and Holly saw Amy's relieved face as she climbed out.

'We got 'em!' yelled Amy. 'We got *all* of them!'

The K.I.D.Z. were in Josh's house later that evening. Mr Hamilton sat on the sofa while the three friends sat in a ring on the floor to count up their car-washing money.

'Not bad,' said Holly, looking at the neat piles of coins. 'Not bad for a couple of days' work. Three burglars *and* all this money.'

All in all, it had been a very successful day. They had all given interviews to the police that afternoon. The raid on Square Deal had caught Gary, and a brief search in the back of the shop had uncovered the rest of the stolen stuff.

Mr Hamilton shook his head. 'I just wish you'd told me what you were doing,' he said. 'You could have got yourselves into a lot of trouble.'

'We didn't know it was burglars,' explained Holly. 'If we'd known *that*, we'd have told someone.'

'So what exactly were you doing in that house?' Mr Hamilton asked.

The three friends looked at one another. This

was going to be quite a lengthy explanation.

They were saved by the doorbell.

'You can tell me all about it in a minute,' said Mr Hamilton. He smiled and shook his head. 'Although whether I'm going to understand it, is another matter.' He got up and went to answer the door.

'It was a good job I remembered where I'd seen Gary before,' said Josh. 'Fancy us buying our DVD from the shop where all the stolen stuff was being kept. And Gary actually served us!'

'You'd have saved us a lot of trouble if you'd remembered that a bit earlier,' said Amy.

'It was the baseball cap,' said Josh. 'I couldn't see him properly. Anyway, I remembered in time, didn't I? They were all caught.'

Amy giggled. 'Poor old Sparky,' she said. 'I bet he had a headache when he came round.'

'It serves him right,' said Holly. 'It serves all of them right.' She grinned. 'People should know better than to tangle with the K.I.D.Z.'

'Does anyone fancy watching a DVD?' said Josh. 'I've hired a good one.' He put a DVD in the machine and pressed the remote control.

'Yess!' Holly and Amy chorused as the credits

rolled. It was their favourite TV programme, *Spyglass*.

'I didn't even know it was on DVD,' said Holly as she settled down to watch.

'It's only just come out,' said Josh.

They had hardly got past the opening titles when Mr Hamilton came back in, his face grim. A policewoman followed him into the room.

'Hello,' said Amy. 'What now?' Her face lit up. 'I know,' she said. 'There's a reward! Is that it?'

'I'm afraid not,' said the policewoman. 'We have reason to believe that your DVD player is stolen property.' She looked at Mr Hamilton. 'You did buy it from the shop called Square Deal in Croftleigh Road, didn't you, sir?'

'Yes,' said Mr Hamilton. 'I'm afraid I did. Josh, it doesn't look like we'll be watching anything this evening. I think the police want our DVD player.'

'I'm afraid so,' said the policewoman. 'I'm very sorry about this.'

The DVD player was disconnected and the policewoman took it away.

'What a rotten trick!' said Josh as the three friends sat staring at the space where the DVD player had been. 'And after all we've done!'

'Oh well,' Holly said with a rueful smile. 'You can't win them all. And we did catch the burglars, didn't we?'

Mr Hamilton came back into the room.

'Will you get your money back, Dad?' asked Josh.

'I don't know,' said Mr Hamilton. 'She said they'd be in touch.' He looked at the unhappy faces of the three friends. 'Don't worry about it,' he said. 'It's not the end of the world. It'll teach me to be a bit more careful about who I buy second-hand DVDs from in future.'

'So,' sighed Amy. 'What now?'

Holly picked up the *Spyglass* DVD. 'I suppose we could watch it at my house,' she said.

Josh looked at his father. 'Would that be OK?' he asked.

Mr Hamilton smiled. 'Of course it would. Off you go. Although, considering the things you three get up to, I'm surprised you need to watch programmes about secret agents!'

Holly laughed. 'It gives us all sorts of new ideas for catching criminals,' she said.

'I think you've caught enough crooks for one

day,' said Mr Hamilton. 'Don't get involved in anything else, please!'

'Of course we won't,' said Holly. 'What could possibly happen between here and my house?'

'With you?' Amy said, laughing. 'Anything!'

Meet Holly, Josh and Amy – Kids in the Danger Zone!

Holly, Josh and Amy are three ordinary kids – with a special talent for solving mysteries. This can be a risky business – but you can bet that the K.I.D.Z. will be having fun at all times!

Look out for these other exciting titles:

Treasure Hunt

How far would you go
for stolen treasure?

A suitcase full of money – stolen, then lost!
But not for long now Holly, Amy and Josh
are on the trail.

Kidnap!

Wasps as a secret weapon?

A local businessman's daughter has been kidnapped. Amy is sure she's seen her but the police won't believe her. It's time for the K.I.D.Z. to use all the tricks they know to solve the crime!

Hostage!

A deadly race against time!

A tent, miles of open country to explore
– and a mystery to solve. Sounds like the
perfect holiday for the K.I.D.Z. Just what
is going on in the strange house on the
moor? Maybe the K.I.D.Z. have bitten off
more than they can chew…